WHEN THE HABOOB SINGS

WHEN THE HABOOB SINGS

A Novel

NEJOUD AL-YAGOUT

gatekeeper press
Columbus, Ohio

This book is a work of fiction. The names, characters and events in this book are the products of the author's imagination or are used fictitiously. Any similarity to real persons living or dead is coincidental and not intended by the author.

When the Haboob Sings

Published by Gatekeeper Press
2167 Stringtown Rd, Suite 109
Columbus, OH 43123-2989
www.GatekeeperPress.com

Copyright © 2019 by Nejoud Al-Yagout
All rights reserved. Neither this book, nor any parts within it may be sold or reproduced in any form or by any electronic or mechanical means, including information storage and retrieval systems without permission in writing from the author. The only exception is by a reviewer, who may quote short excerpts in a review.

ISBN (hardcover): 9781642376098
ISBN (paperback): 9781642376081
eISBN: 9781642376074

Printed in the United States of America

HOW DID I get here? How did I become a prisoner in a cell? This here cell, my transient home. This here cell, which I will try to describe to you. People treasure descriptions, do they not? I have been here in this place long enough to describe it pretty well for years to come, and it is easy for me to do so now, as I am here, inside it. In this cell with its rusty bars, a window I cannot reach, and the sun's rays beating down on the dust-filled corner of the room. This cell, with its leaky faucet, a sink with peeling skin beneath its waist, a squat toilet, a showerhead dangling from a plastic hose, grey-tiled floors (or maybe faded black), and smelling of urine and Dettol.

Here I stand, kneel, lie down, and walk around, with fists clenched and muscles tightened, glancing around at my home of the last two months with cockroaches for roommates. Last night there were two. One of them is dead now: I beat it with the shoe of the cleaning lady who brought my dinner last night. She was too scared to kill it herself. The other one is lingering around, its antennae swaying, dancing to a beat I cannot hear, making its way slowly, ever so slowly, toward my bare feet that are much in need of a pedicure, might I add. I need a shoe. The wardens took my slippers away when I first came here. Do not ask me why. They can hardly be used as weapons. And besides, I would not use a weapon even if I had one; violence is not in my core. At least, I do not think it is. I read once that we all have violent tendencies, and in moments of survival or protecting our loved ones, they rage to the surface. I do not want to think about that right now.

I am less restless than I was earlier this morning. I always wake up nervous here, with heart palpitations, sweaty skin, and even tremors sometimes. I am well taken care of, but the sense of anticipation of leaving this hellhole grips me each and every day. However, after I splash my face with water and brush my teeth, I feel better. Something about water, something.

Here I am sitting on the makeshift bed, a mattress with holes, a haven for bedbugs. Oh, in that case, I must have more unwelcome roommates! There is a sorry excuse for a bedcover and a thin, flimsy off-white bed-sheet. The pillow has no case. There is a prayer mat, with a praying robe that I have not touched, but on nights when I feel cold, I slip into the robe and sleep in it.

Here I am, bent over, and resting my chin upon my knees. I am too scared to kill the cockroach today. That is the thing when it comes to killing insects, for me at least: sometimes I have the courage, and sometimes the fear is overwhelming. I can feel the fear reverberating inside of me. Constricted throat, shortness of breath, yes. But I can pat myself on the back for having killed one of them. That is an accomplishment. It is now a battle between this one and me. I am vying for sole occupancy.

WHEN THE HABOOB SINGS

Once in a while, a mouse passes by. On nights when my chest hurts because the anxiety is overwhelming, I wait for the pitter-patter of feet, not out of loneliness, but out of sheer terror that I will wake up to a mouse staring me in the face. *Best to stay awake*, I tell myself when the paranoia engulfs me. But sleep always wins in the end, and so far I have not woken up to a mouse on my bed, thank God.

I watch the cockroach walk slowly, stop, walk slowly, stop, walk—nay, glide—toward the bars and make its exit. At this moment in time, a cockroach has more dignity, more freedom than me. A cockroach has the right to leave. And I, a human being, am confined to a cell, at the mercy and whim of my fellow men.

But let me ask again, for your sake, of course: how did I get here?

Well, to answer that, we must go back in time. Say, two years? Yes, that is about right. That is not when the writing started. Oh, I have not told you about that yet. Sorry, my brain is so scattered sometimes. I have mentioned the insects and the mouse before I even introduced myself. Yes, I am a writer, a published one at that: I have not written novels or poetry, or any kind of book so to speak, but I have written articles. I started writing when I was fourteen, and publicly when I was twenty-five, for local magazines and newspapers. (Be patient, I will hint at my country of birth soon.) I am now thirty-two. That is eighteen years of writing, and seven—going on eight—years of sharing my work with the public. I know age matters. I will be the first to admit that I always want to know someone's age. Whether or not a person's age *should* matter, though, is beyond me: I have never found an answer that did not lead to another question. But I never ask an adult. It is considered impolite, no? Anyway, I am thirty-two years of age, and it was only a couple of years ago when my writing started getting attention.

Before becoming famous (or infamous, depending on your view of my story), I wrote about the environment, I wrote about hobbies, I wrote about voting, and I wrote about education. But something inside me, or outside me, was shaping my destiny, nudging me toward the path of writing about subjects that were unwritten about where I live. However, at the time, I was too afraid to venture beyond what was considered safe writing. All my articles had been safe, but it was that day in a room filled with men that things changed. Perhaps you are wondering what is unsafe in terms of writing? Well, in my country, it is best to stay away from two topics: politics and religion. Unless, of course, you are showering politicians and religion with praise. To be fair, my first foray into unsafe writing was neither about politics nor religion, but about gender equality. Still, in a patriarchy, anything regarding women is teetering on the domain of politics and religion.

So, in just one night I went from being a safe writer to an unsafe one. There I was, sitting at an all-male gathering, the only woman. I heard them speak of the weather—*yawn!*—poets—*interesting*—and women's stupidity—*the nerve!*—and I inhaled loudly. And exhaled even more loudly. A couple of men glared at me, as though challenging me to say something. My husband, Adam, shot me a look. He wanted me to be quiet. I closed my eyes. I kept them shut for a bit too long.

But before I relate what happened next, I know you want to imagine the surroundings, but I must confess that I do not notice my surroundings much. And it was two years ago. It was easy for me to describe the cell because I live here now. Perhaps I am self-engrossed. Or maybe it is because I have always associated homes and places and even people with feelings. I am good at remembering how I felt, what a person said, or how he or she moved. I can even imitate someone's voice and gestures. I often entertained my family by imitating others, but I stopped years ago when my family bought a parrot that embarrassed me in front of an aunt by imitating me imitating her. The parrot's imitations of me imitating my aunt included shrill laughter and chortling. The aunt did not say anything, but she flushed and the consequent silence was too awkward for everyone at the family gathering. The parrot died years later, and we never bought another one.

Yes, voices and gestures come easy to me. But describing a scene, clothing, or a location? Not so easy. I once visited a house with black walls. Jet black walls. Now that is not hard to describe. Just imagine black walls. Not the entire house, just a room in it. I mean, how can anyone forget that? And how can anyone not notice black walls? I was at the house of a girl called Rayan who I was paired with—was it eleventh or twelfth grade?—in Biology. We were studying the habits of rats, and she told me to meet her at her house after school. And that is when she led me to her room with the black walls.

Anyway, back to that all-male gathering. To this day, I have no idea if they wanted me to hear or if they accidentally mentioned it, forgetting a woman was in the room. But come on. How could they not have noticed me? I was an anomaly. You see, these gatherings are our society's versions of "man caves." Most houses have an extension built especially for men to meet and discuss politics. Women are not generally welcome, although years ago my father mentioned a woman who held co-ed gatherings. Iconic, huh?

I felt awkward the moment my husband and I greeted the men in the cave. One man refused to shake my hand. I asked my husband later whether it was because he was religious, and he nodded.

When the conversation turned to women's stupidity, things turned ugly fast. I, the writer, who does not speak much in public, had to say something, right? I mean, I could not just sit there while they insulted women.

There they were, dressed in long white robes from head to toe, with white headgear secured in place by black rings on the crowns of their heads. There they were, snickering about a woman candidate in Parliament, scoffing about women who think they are fit to make legislation. There they were, mocking a female singer. *She wears tight shirts to flaunt her breasts and gain fans*, one said. There they were, agreeing among themselves that women were their downfall and that they wished the female population would stick to shopping, raising children, and wearing makeup while leaving men to business, politics, and running the world. There they were, and there I was, fuming.

WHEN THE HABOOB SINGS

I pointed my finger at them and began to address the all-male congregation. And to the best of my memory, I said something like this: "How dare you! Women have been in Parliament for over eleven years here, and it is about time you got used to it! Why are you clinging so tightly to the patriarchy? What intimidates you about women? Why are you competing with us? Without women, you would not exist..."

And I *blah blah blah*ed my way through, my face hot and red, beads of sweat traveling down my forehead, stinging my eyes. I could not stop *blah blah*ing, even when the room turned black for a millisecond (have you ever been so nervous you could not see?), even when I had to catch my breath. I, the introvert, the shy one, expressed myself in a room filled with men. The tirade went on for about a minute or two. A few were looking at the ground, ashamed at themselves, others were looking at the ground, ashamed of me, but most of them were glaring menacingly at me or casting glances at my husband, Adam, waiting for him to react, to say something, *anything*.

I was about to go on when one of the men coughed, cleared his throat, and addressed Adam: "If you can't control your wife, you shouldn't bring her here."

"My name is Dunya," I said.

He did not even turn to look at me but added, facing my husband, "In fact, I think you should take her home now. You are always welcome here, but she isn't."

I was not even supposed to go to this all-male gathering, but my husband and I were invited to his parents' house for dinner, and since they lived near the men's parlor, and we lived across town, he suggested I accompany him so he did not have to come back home again to pick me up. I told him I could drive myself and meet him at his parents' place, but he wanted me to accompany him.

I answered, "But they're all men." I remember saying that. I remember not wanting to go. I should have listened to my intuition.

Adam told me, "We'll only be there for half an hour. I have to show my face. And you're with me, so nobody can say anything. I've known these guys forever. They won't mind."

When we arrived, I was still reticent. I insisted that I could wait in the car, but we both agreed it was too hot, and that was that. After we left, he ignored me in the car. And we had a tense dinner at his parents' house. When we got back home, we got into an argument. I asked him why he did not defend me in front of his friends, and he told me I did not understand the men of our culture. He did not want to be referred to as a steering wheel, a derogatory term reserved for men who had no personality and were under the thumbs of their wives. After we argued back and forth, back and forth, he said he was tired, and he kissed my forehead (I remember that clearly) and we went to sleep.

When I woke up the next morning, I felt compelled to do something. Confronting the men at the gathering had not been enough for me. And that was that. I wrote about what had happened the night before. I, the writer, the contributor, who had stuck to op-eds related to news articles and safe subjects, shifted toward a social issue, and though I had not yet broached an absolutely unsafe topic, I knew this would ruffle feathers. I wrote and wrote about gender inequality, double standards, hypocrisy, judgment. I, the writer, used the pen, or the keyboard in this case, and poured my heart into that article. Not to condemn men, but to beg them to stop: stop harassing us, stop imposing, stop dictating, stop berating, stop intimidating, stop controlling, just stop, stop, stop!

I, the writer, expanded the article and wrote of the exhaustion of women all across the globe protecting ourselves, carrying sprays in our tiny purses, and constantly looking over our shoulders. I wrote about the men who looked down on us and subjugated us, who abused us and discriminated against us. And, to be fair, I thanked the men who supported us, the men who, like us, were tired of the patriarchy.

MY MAILBOX quickly filled up. Men criticizing, men supporting, women agreeing, whining about their husbands, their veils, their woes, their pressures, women condemning me, fans agreeing, followers lamenting, and I, the writer, responded to each and every one of them. I remember one person tagged me on social media exclaiming her excitement that I, the writer, was humble enough to respond to her and thank her for her support. Her post was an excerpt of my response—without my permission, but who was I to say anything to someone who was publicly praising me?—and the caption was filled with hearts and more hearts. Although there were only about twenty emails, it was my first taste of celebrity, and the attention galvanized me.

The week after the gender equality article, I wrote an article asking why children of local women married to expatriates had no citizenship. Why, I wrote, did local men who married women from other countries automatically pass their citizenship on to their offspring? I added that it was unfair of the state to ask potential spouses from other religions to convert to Islam. Why should anyone interfere in something as personal as marriage? If women here want to get married to others outside the faith, I wrote, that should be between them and their husbands. Why does the state prefer that both parents are Muslim? Why can a local Muslim man marry a Christian or a Jew, but a local Muslim woman can only marry a Muslim?

Here is something I did not include in the article: I know a local Muslim woman who married a Christian. He pretended to convert to have their marriage recognized by the state, but he remained a devout Christian. People were asking whether this man, in his early thirties, got circumcised! The bride said yes, but that was an outright lie. It does not bother anyone whether a person has truly converted or not. In any case, he becomes a poster child for conversion, another headcount in the statistics of Muslims in the world.

Here is another thing I did not include in the article: My friend Layla has an aunt who married a Coptic man from Egypt. Her aunt had secretly become a Coptic as well. During one of the gentleman's visits back home to Alexandria, as he was praying in a church, bombs exploded. At the hospital, he begged the doctors not to reveal his identity for fear of backlash from his wife's family. He came back here without a limb and to this day everyone thinks he had been in a car accident. Can you imagine not being able to recount such an important incident in one's life? To suffer in silence? To have to live a lie like that because one's religion might be offensive or against the marital law? Layla's aunt only revealed the truth to Layla, and when Layla relayed the story to me I could not stop crying.

Anyway, back to my article, the one that touched a nerve among the public, the one about marrying outside the faith. A renowned local cleric berated me on social media. He addressed me by name and tagged me, stating in his post: "Dunya, the reason the state interferes with the religion of the spouse is because everyone in the world should be Muslim. And that is that. Be careful, you are treading on the grounds of infidels."

And just like that, I was famous. A popular local cleric was aware of my writing and had addressed me directly. He knew who I was. This was a man known for his radical views. And now his Twitter feed was flooded with comments liking what he said to me. I waited a couple of hours to respond and finally commented: "Thank you for your view. I appreciate your feedback."

To which he responded: "I have a sermon on Thursday about the beauty of Islam. Please join us. It will enlighten you."

And I replied: "Thank you for the invitation." Although I did not add: "I can't make it." Or, "I won't be there, not interested." I did not need someone telling me about the beauty of religion. Especially not someone with radical views.

I got to reading emails. I glimpsed through some of them and read others intently. But the response that struck out for me the most was from someone who called himself Mr. X, who addressed his email as a thank you letter and began in a pleasant tone that swiftly turned caustic.

WHEN THE HABOOB SINGS

To: Dunya Khair
From: Mr. X
Subject: Thank you

Hello there Dunya,

I read your article regarding women marrying outside the faith. In your article, you also included that it was unjust that women who marry men from other countries cannot pass citizenship on to their children. I agree with you regarding the latter. My nephew is a victim of this prejudice. My sister married a Jordanian man and my nephew faces the stigma of having a local mother and a foreign father. Although his father is an Arab and a Muslim, he is made fun of at school for his accent and is bullied by boys outside of school for being different. And so I thank you for addressing that.

But the part about marrying a non-Muslim is blasphemous and I wish we lived in a country where you were charged with the appropriate punishment: death. You deserve to die. People like you should not be allowed to roam freely with the living. How dare you!

This is how it starts. First, people like you test the waters by saying it is okay to marry outside the faith. A little time passes, nobody says much, and maybe you will begin to tell people it is okay to have doubts. You might think that is not enough and start to invite others to leave the faith altogether. Finally, you could insult our faith, and what next? It keeps going on and on unless we put an end to it now. Better to kill the virus before it spreads.

Do not consider this a death threat. I value my life too much to threaten you. I value weapons too much to use them on someone as vile and as disgusting and as parasitical as you. I would never spend my time languishing in jail for someone like you, although I hope someone else feels otherwise and makes it his mission to ensure that you disappear from our planet. I hope that person kills you so we put an end to such a vicious attack on our culture. Still, I thank you for making people aware of how diseased we are. You have sparked debates in our country, you have divided us, but you have also made us aware that we are slipping away from our values. You are the tumor we needed to cure our society of the cancer of waywardness.

I know there are thousands like you and killing one person will not do much. But I hope you will become an example for others who dare to follow your footsteps. I hope through your death people will learn to keep their mouths shut.

Do you know what you are? You are a haboob, a dust storm. A destructive haboob that obscures vision. But even the most powerful haboob has no chance but to disappear in time. Even the most powerful haboob is forgotten. And I hope your time is up, Dunya Khair. And I hope that people will forget you, Dunya Khair.

I know the threat of eternal punishment does not terrify you because you do not believe in anything except yourself and your distorted mission to corrupt the minds of people around you. I know you must write to seek supporters and find safety in numbers. But you will never be safe. I hope you know that. Again, I am not threatening you, just expressing my wish to see you pay for what you have done by dying an ignoble death, rotting in the afterlife, you sick woman, you sick, dirty, ugly woman.

I can't even believe I am taking the time out of my day to even write this to you. You do not even deserve a second of my time or anyone's time.

I thank you again and again for reminding us that there is an illness we need to recover from fast.

From someone who hates you with a hatred that surpasses even his own capability for hatred,

Mr. X

I read and reread the email again and again. I checked my phone. Four missed calls from Adam. I called him back and told him about the exchange with the cleric and I read him the email from Mr. X.

"Sick people out there. Sick. Try not to read your emails baby. Just write your articles and forget about all the feedback." That is what my Adam said to me. He added that I have his respect and support and, to me, that is all that mattered.

Adam and I were a team, fighting and making up, yelling at one another and calming each other down. It was an arranged marriage, which is surprising for someone as liberal as me—I know, I know. But I never tried dating, even though I got married fairly late for my society, a couple of years shy of my thirtieth birthday. A few guys had approached me before Adam and tried to get my number, but I ignored them.

I was too scared to have a boyfriend because I did not want to go through the stress of worrying whether or not a man was serious about marrying me. I also did not want to get caught by my parents.

When I graduated from university at the age of twenty-one, I asked my mom to find a husband for me. Mom, in turn, asked her friend, who asked her friend and after seven years—yes, seven!—of searching for a suitable life partner, I was introduced to Adam, the son of my father's business partner's cousin's acquaintance. Mama's friends and relatives had introduced me to many men throughout the years, but I rejected each of them, even though many of them were eager to propose. My mother warned me that I would be a spinster if I continued being picky, but I wanted a life partner, not social validation. And it was this patience that led me to Adam.

Adam and I clicked at first sight. Our mothers left us alone in the living room of Adam's family home, and we spoke for two hours with our chaperones sitting patiently in the adjacent reception area. The marriage was rushed. I was twenty-eight and he was thirty-five. We were not in love, but we were drawn to each other. We spent hours on the phone and never ran out of things to say. And as a result, I do not think anyone saw any reason for delay.

I remember him confessing he was an atheist during our engagement, half expecting me to break it off. And though at that point I had privately renounced my religion too, I was a lover of God, and so I tried to convince him that God exists and he tried to convince me otherwise. At some point during the courtship, we grew tired of debating and agreed to disagree, avoiding the topic altogether.

When we first got married, I was surprised to learn that my atheist husband was a devout worshipper in public who walked to the mosque every Friday with our neighbors. But instead of criticizing him, I woke him up half an hour before the call to prayer.

For a few months, he stopped going to the mosque altogether. But he resumed going after my article defending local women who want to marry non-Muslims. I suppose he did not want people to know he agreed with me.

After writing about gender equality, and about why women here cannot marry non-Muslims, I wrote about the roles of men and women. I wrote of men behind closed doors and in the public eye. I wrote about why men will not defend their wives in public, how they are afraid to be referred to as steering wheels, and why it is important that men stand up for us, so we are no longer subjugated. I hit the send button and woke up the next day to my cell phone ringing. It was Adam. I wanted to read the emails before answering his call. I was sure he was angry and I wanted to distract myself. There were many unread emails. I scrolled down and saw an email from Mr. X. I did not open it and reported it as spam. Goodbye Mr. X. I randomly picked emails to read and spam. I was tired of the hate. Why even bother getting in touch if you hate me so much? One man verbally harassed me in his email, calling me vulgar and inane, there was an email from a woman who said I do not represent the fairer sex (is that not considered a derogatory phrase these days?), and an email from a famous local marriage counselor who said that, as a wife with duties and responsibilities, I was not honoring the sanctity of marriage.

Adam called back again. I answered this time.

"It sounds like you are talking about me in your latest article. Dammit D," he said.

"Well," I responded, "I have to start my op-eds from something that affects me personally, and yes, in some cases, our conversations, recent and past, inspire me."

The reaction to this article got progressively more intense. I lost count of the emails that arrived all day and all night. Several people declared me a feminist, as though it were an insult. I did not consider myself one, far from it. And though I had written back-to-back articles defending women, I did not deserve the label.

And because they called me a feminist, I started changing the subjects, as I did not want to be confined to a label. I wrote among other things about road rage, censorship, youth activism, political correctness, cultural appropriation, our invisible caste system, the far left and the far right, distribution of wealth, democracy, and finally, I wrote about apostasy. Two years after establishing myself as a somewhat controversial writer who always left room for loopholes, for *no, I didn't mean that, it's open for interpretation* in every piece, I finally wrote about leaving religion. And you cannot find a loophole in that.

One by one, each of the papers to which I had submitted the article rejected it, saying it was offensive or too sensitive, even *dangerous, aren't you afraid this will get you in trouble?* But I was not afraid. Not one bit. I held no claims over the right path, but I knew the path that was right for *me*. And I wanted to defend myself, and others, who were on this path. I wanted to give a voice to the voiceless.

"Apostasy is a crime, and you will be persecuted. It is a duty for them to persecute you," one editor said to me over the phone.

"Well, this is my viewpoint," I retorted.

"Your viewpoint is filled with contempt," he said, right before hanging up on me.

How rude! I felt afraid, not for my life, but that I was being judged for hating a religion I did not hate. I had nothing against Islam. It brought me up, it took care of me, it held my hand, and it sheltered me when storms were raging within and without me. How could I hate it? It would be like hating a nanny who raised me. But I grew afraid of my nanny. There was the constant threat of abuse and a lifetime of agony if I did not obey. I noticed all the other nannies were the same, so I could not hire another one, nor did I need one anymore. Each one, in her own way, had a set of rules: Iron your clothes, lay them out on your bed in the morning, go to sleep early, brush your teeth, take a shower at this time, go out on this day, and do not ever complain. Ever. "And don't worry," the nanny whispered in a menacing tone, "if you obey me, I will make your bed and cook for you. If you do not obey me, though, I will throw you out of the house to sleep on the streets and then cook you in a boiling pot. For eternity."

WHAT IS this thing we have about wanting to come out? Why do we feel the need to announce our sexuality, our faith (or lack of it), our political inclinations, our likes and dislikes publicly? Why? And why do some people want us to keep our views private?

I grappled with these questions while receiving one rejection after another for the apostasy article. But the question beneath all the questions racing in my mind was: When will someone brave enough come forth and publish my article? And so it happened that a brave editor came forth and agreed to publish my article in his paper, a renowned local paper to boot. He warned me of the risks, but the owner, a famous and respected businessman, was willing to gamble on me. "The worst they can do is put us in jail and close down the paper transiently," he said.

And so, the article was published. And it went viral. Right away. My mother said to me: "You should have told us you were going to write this article, but Baba is proud of you, and he wants you to know he supports you all the way."

"What about you, Mama?" I asked. She insisted she supported me too but wished she had known about it first.

"Would you have stopped me, Mama?"

"No, of course not," she said, "but if you had told me, I would have been prepared."

"Prepared for what?" I asked.

"Prepared for the slaughter, Dunya. Prepared for the slaughter."

"What slaughter?" I asked.

"People's tongues, Dunya. You know how small our society is, and they will slaughter you and everyone connected to you with their tongues. Still," she added, "you are my child and I will support you all the way. And it's an outstanding article. Much-needed."

Mama is what one would call a traditional conservative. She has been to Mecca and fasts in Ramadan. She does not pray daily, does not believe in an afterlife, and is convinced that man has tainted all the prophets' messages. Baba is not religious at all. He pretends to believe, but I overheard him on the phone once telling someone that the planet would be better off without religion. And he pretends to fast in Ramadan, although the cook once admitted to me that he secretly brings meals to Baba in his office. I am sure Mama knew about this. He would not have been able to ask the cook to prepare dishes without her finding out. So, if we are a product of our surroundings, it is accurate to conclude that the seed of apostasy was planted in me as a child, albeit unintentionally, by a mother who picks and chooses the parts of the faith that resonate with her, and a father who is a closet unbeliever.

We were taught to pray by my maternal grandmother, and my paternal grandfather encouraged us to

WHEN THE HABOOB SINGS

fast. My immediate family barely brought religion up. It was only mentioned in the presence of devout relatives. My brother, my sister, and I were mostly left to our own devices, and I mean that literally: television, video games, and the technology du jour. My sister Alia was the only one in the family who prayed. And that was her choice. But Mama and Baba cared about what society thought of us and told us never to tell people we did not pray.

MY APOSTASY article garnered thousands of responses, countless death threats, and even a warning letter from a lawyer sent to me and copied to the paper calling to remove it and apologize publicly. And lo and behold! A mere ten minutes after the email was sent, the article disappeared from the web, although thankfully, no public apology was issued. After the article was removed, I posted it on my personal blog, which crashed for a few hours because of the number of people visiting my site. Another warning letter came from the same lawyer telling me he knew it was on my blog and that I had better remove it or I would face serious consequences. Was he cyber-stalking me? I did not remove the article.

Then a phone call arrived. There were fifty—yes, fifty—lawsuits against me. The phone call was from the Ministry, claiming that I had broken the law by insulting religion and reminding me that apostasy was a crime. I informed him that I was not insulting religion by discussing my personal journey and that I harbored no ill will for anyone. I asked him where my rights as a writer were. "What about freedom of speech?" I asked. He repeated that I had broken the law and should be aware of the limitation on my rights and that I was given enough freedom to discuss other subjects but should have stayed away from blasphemy. I told him apostasy and blasphemy are two different things, to which he responded that both were crimes. He asked me why I thought it was important to tell people I was an apostate? Did I court scandal? I told him that in our world we have women's rights, gay rights, and workers' rights. But what about apostates' rights?

Had I merely written in vague terms about apostasy, I would not have been in trouble, he said, refusing to tell me his name when I asked. And having informed me that the line was recorded, the Ministry representative asked me: "Do you, Dunya, continue to insist you are an apostate?" I told the man that it was easy for me to lie and say I was not one in order to avoid trouble or dissuade further threats, but I believed in honesty, integrity, and remaining true to who I was.

He asked me again: "So are you saying you are still an apostate?"

To which I responded: "Well, obviously, I am not so unstable that I would write about being an apostate and now tell you I am not."

He said: "But you are unstable enough to leave Islam?"

I told him I was done with this conversation, and because I was being recorded, added: "Thank you for calling. I expect to hear from you soon."

Although I retained a sense of calm during the phone call, I found myself trembling when I hung up the phone. I had to sit down and catch my breath. *What are they going to do to me?* I thought. I immediately went online. My supporters called me brave, and those who were against me called me a coward, a weak soul who had succumbed to the whisperings of the evil one. And some trolls called me cruel. Now, I can understand being called brave or a coward, but cruel? But I understood where the fear was coming from. Many people become apostates because of hatred of religion, even hatred of believers. But I have not an ounce of hate for Islam or Muslims.

Nothing, to me, could match the freedom of not belonging to anything. Of course, there were moments when I wished I did belong, but I never quite belonged to anything. I was never part of a crowd at school, and I never experienced the camaraderie of colleagues at an office. God bless my country. Not that there is anything wrong with working, but for someone shy like me, who would not have been able to function around others, I feel relieved that oil was discovered and my grandfather capitalized on the discovery by founding a business selling tankers to oil companies—that is beyond lucrative, in case you are wondering. I am also glad I do not have to work so I do not have to deal with gushing fans or vicious haters at a water cooler. Oh, and glaring eyes.

I can hide from eyes, but I cannot escape technology. The threats grew, but my husband had become a vocal enthusiast of my cause, shedding his layers of hypocrisy by tweeting on my behalf, rallying support for my apostasy, stopping short only of confessing his own disbelief. They blocked my social media, they blocked my blog, they blocked my website, they blocked my YouTube channel (although all of Adam's friends who lived abroad said the sites were not blocked in their respective countries). I spent many a day at my parents' house reading comments of support and comments from those saying I should be arrested. I was aware of those defending me and of the ones condemning me on social media, and the ones who vacillated between loving and hating me. I had sparked a war between those who were fighting for freedom of speech and those who were clinging to ideology.

Even as an apostate, some things stayed with me. And are still with me today. I still prostrate to God in moments of gratitude. I still read verses of the Koran aloud when I am afraid. I still find beautiful passages about our Creator that leave me awestruck. I still say "Praise to Allah" and mean it. I do not drink alcohol. I do not eat pork. I still believe that a physical relationship should only be between two spouses. In a way, I will always be a Muslim, so you might ask why I consider myself an apostate. It is because I do not want to believe that God puts us in hell for what we eat or drink or what we do or which gender we love or how we worship. I do not want to believe in a God who has created hell. Period. And even if all the hatred against gays and infidels and idolaters in scripture is real, I do not want to be a part of it. And not wanting to be a part of it any longer makes me an apostate. And unlike religious people, I do not claim to know who God is. Instead, I say: "God, I hope you're not the God of religion, of any religion. I hope you are who I hope you are."

Still, these are my beliefs that I will never impose on others. I, the writer, merely write and express myself. Who am I to think I am on a right path? I am on a path that is right for *me*, but that does not mean it is right for others or even the right path at all. But my path, the right one for me, was and is apostasy.

The thing with apostasy is that it is never an overnight decision. Nor is it something to take lightly. The mind is not idle, and it will fight you. If you are religious, it will give you reasons not to be. It will tempt you, torture you with blasphemous thoughts, and tell you to leave the fold; and if you are irreligious, it will condemn you to hellfire, call you a sinner, and tell you to repent and return to religion.

But I could not handle my hypocrisy, and the voice inside of me got louder and louder. It no longer mattered whether it was an angel or a devil talking to me. The only thing that mattered was renouncing my religion. But before I plunged into the ocean of apostasy, I had many conversations with God. One day I remember taking a walk outside my home and bawling, asking God who He was. I asked for a sign. And the call to prayer came on suddenly! I even saw Allah's name on a billboard once when I was thinking of Him while driving. But signs that apostasy was the right path came as well and were also displayed on billboards (the word *freedom* when I asked God if I should leave religion and be free, now come on!) or coming through speakers on my laptop in the form of videos proving dogma was manmade and debates revealing contradictions in scripture. In the end, apostasy won. And my desire to publicize it could no longer be contained.

WEEKS PASSED. And the drumroll sounded in the form of a doorbell at my marital residence.

A search warrant was presented, and they came storming in. They raided the house, upturned closets, confiscated our laptops and our desktop. They asked us to turn in our cell phones. They fumbled through drawers, scoured medicine cabinets, even raided the maid's room, the kitchen, and the living room. They looked under carpets and on top of cupboards.

I reassured myself that just because it is against the law to be an apostate does not make it wrong. I did not kill anyone, I did not threaten the state, I did not promote apostasy, and I did not criticize Islam. But how could I explain that to the men in the house I shared with my husband?

Do you know how there is always someone in a crowd who is in charge? You can just tell. In my house on that fateful day, I knew exactly who was in charge. He was the one pointing, barking orders, and telling the men where to look and what to look for. He had black boots with khaki pants tucked into them, and he kept giving me the dirtiest looks. He had a bloated belly and puffed-up chest and made me feel uneasy. And I know he wanted to.

After nearly three hours of searching, the man in charge walked toward me. I was pushed to the ground and handcuffed.

I remember screaming in protest while being held down. I remember a flurry of feet and boots on the marble floor. I remember the room turning dark and waking up at a police station. There were questions, so many questions.

"I have the right to a lawyer," I said.

The response: "Listen to this one! Who wants to defend an infidel?"

It was not one man who said that, it was a chorus of them.

And the chorus persisted: "You, the infidel, you. The one who left behind Paradise for this Earth. The one who succumbed to the whisperings of the evil one. You, who deserve a wretched fate, may you rot in prison, may you rot in hell, you! Nobody will defend someone as filthy as you. Cursed infidel, filthy apostate, you!"

"I am not an infidel," I remember saying. "I believe in God! Leave me alone! I want a lawyer. I want my mom!"

"Your *mom*? Your mom has denounced you publicly. She wants nothing to do with you." It was him, the scary policeman, he of the bushy eyebrows and chipmunk cheeks. The leader.

"That's a lie! I just spoke to her last night! I want to speak to my mom!" I shrilled.

"It is not a lie. They have released a statement this morning and disowned you. Now you have to sign these papers renouncing your apostasy for them to come back to you. Otherwise, you'll be stuck in prison for a long time and there will be no inheritance for you."

"Nobody will block my inheritance. By Sharia law—"

"Ah, the defiant infidel speaks of Sharia law when it suits her. The selfish infidel, the shame to our society, cares only about money, using Islam for her benefit. See? She doesn't cry for her family. She just focused on the word inheritance. Selfish infidel! Vile creature! What do you expect from someone who turns away from God? Your family has cut you off. You are nothing to them. Persona non grata." At that, he spit on the floor and left.

And the chorus sang on, a medley of both sopranos and altos: "Nobody loves you. Your husband has deleted his Twitter account and apologized to the public. He will divorce you as soon as you are out of jail."

I imagined the policemen dancing, walking from left to right, orchestrated, the strophe—or was it the antistrophe?—fox-trotting, delirious, a synchronized march. After which they all turned toward me, waiting for my response so they could sing again, in all their glory.

"Jail? You can't send me to jail without a court case!"

Snickering, more snickering. I even witnessed a policeman high fiving another policeman.

"Too many movies," the chorus chanted. "Too many ideas about freedom and democracy and liberty and freedom! Dangerous thinking. Western ideals. What happens to people who leave their culture? They wither away and die. You tried your best to cause division in our country. But we are here to show you the strong arm of the law."

They asked me to sign the paper renouncing my apostasy again. I declined. One of the cops led me to the cell: the cell I am in now, without toilet paper, with a toothbrush encased in plastic (thankfully unused), and a used, odorless bar of soap. There was no shampoo.

I asked a policeman why there was no shampoo. He looked at the other policemen and said: "She asks for shampoo. The silly infidel asks for shampoo." And they all began to laugh, to roar, to howl.

And he added: "What is the soap for, stupid?"

"I use soap for my body and my face. Not my hair," I retorted.

"No, silly woman. It is for your body, your face, and your hair. Do you think you have come to a five-star resort? You threw away all your blessings. Look where you are. This is your abode now. Shall we order bath products for you, your highness? You should be grateful you are not being hanged. And while you are at it, use the soap to wash your mind! Wash all the thoughts right out of that filthy mind of yours. Wash the devil out and surrender to God. Say *La Ilaha Illa Allah*."

And I said: "*La Ilaha Illaha Allah*." There is no God but Allah.

He asked how I could say *La Ilaha Illa Allah* when I was an apostate.

To which I replied: "I don't need to be a Muslim to believe in Allah."

SO NOW, here we are. In the cell with three walls and rusty bars for the fourth. Outside, through the bars, I can see a concrete wall. Down the hallway, past the heavy bolted metal door, is the police station. I cannot see it, but I know it is there because that is the door I came in from. There is no indication of other cells, no voices, and no sound except for when they bring me my food or when one of the cleaning ladies warns me that policemen are on their way to see me, coming to check on me, trying to ascertain whether my time here has changed my mind. It has not. If anything, it has strengthened my convictions.

Yes, here we are. Shall we move on from the cell to where I am from, where I live, where the cell and I are located? Let us refer to it as an unnamed Muslim country in Arabia, a desert on a coastline. It is a small country bordering the country that hosts Mecca and Medina to the south and the Hanging Gardens of Babylon to the north. It is located in the Arabian Gulf. We Arabs do not call it the Persian Gulf.

The capital city, which along with the word *city* boasts the same name as the country, is a desert oasis with high-rise luxury buildings, glossy financial centers, malls, malls, and more malls, petroleum rigs, shanties and run-down buildings, surrounded by suburbs of glittery mansions and not so glittery concrete houses—some with sapphire blue double-glazed windows and aluminum panes—fancy apartment complexes and not so fancy ones, modern and dilapidated structures, assuming and unassuming. Surrounding the suburbs are uninhabited areas of sand and dunes, palm trees, desert shrubs, and inhabited areas of tents and compounds. The national flower is the *arfaj*. Oh here come the tears. Tears of love for my country. Yes, love. Even from within the confines of a cell. Because regardless of what many people think, I love my country. It is my unwavering faith in my country's potential that I find hope and solace in my writing.

    I hear shuffling. It is time for dinner. A cheese sandwich, plain, toasted bread. A glass of orange juice. I always have to smell the glass. Once it smelled of dishwashing liquid, and another time it smelled of a wet towel. Today it smells like nothing, which is a relief. My dessert today is a yellow date. I do not feel like eating. I miss my husband. I miss my mother, my father, my sister, and my brother. I miss my best friend, Layla. To stop myself from feeling isolated, I have a secret notepad here. I begged a cleaning lady for a pen and a notepad when I first came here.

    "No, no, no, no," she said over and over again, turning over her shoulder, though nobody was there. *Camera*, she pointed.

    "Yes, but it's not at this angle. You can hide the stationery under your shirt. Find a way."

    "Angle, angle, angle," she repeated. "Yes, not at this angle," she sang as she took over the role of the chorus. I imagined Mr. Head-Officer, in his black boots and khaki pants, twirling her around while she sang: "The camera is not at this angle," to which he responds, also singing: "The camera is everywhere, even when you cannot see it."

The camera was always on her mind and on her tongue. But she relented one day, which made me proud of my powers of persuasion. She brought a cheap red pen. It ran out of ink quickly, but during each of her shifts, she brought me a new one. Under my mattress, there were several pens, green, blue, black, even a pink one with unicorns and a feather, a lime-green feather. When I remember, I remind her to throw away the ones that do not work. Pens normally last eons for me, but in this cell, there is something monstrous in the air sucking the pens dry. Here, in this ink-sucking, claustrophobic cell.

One day, I asked Ms. Cleaning Lady to bring me a newspaper. I could tell from the horrified look on her face that this time, no meant no, and there was no convincing her otherwise.

At least I have a notepad and pens of all colors. Now, I do not write articles. No, sir. No, ma'am. I do not dare. I just doodle on a blank page. Every night before resting my sore back, my stiff neck, or my pounding head on the hard, dirty mattress, I doodle whatever comes to mind: a giraffe, a lake, my mother's portrait, this cell, a dandelion, a locust, even a radiator. Yesterday, I asked the maid to find out how many days I have been in here and she reported back to me a couple of hours later. Sixty-two days. Two months and two days give or take and still counting.

I am going crazy contemplating the injustice of it all: no lawyer, no family visits, and no husband fighting policemen, racing to my cell as they drag him backward by his elbows and his heels scrape the ground. I can imagine him resisting and all of them falling to the ground in a heap. There is my Adam grabbing a key from the pocket of one of the policemen and throwing it through the bars of the cell. I turn the key in the keyhole and open the cell gate and we race off into the vastness of the desert together, leaving all the policemen in a stupor, unable to move until we are out of sight.

Yes, yes, yes. That is my Adam. And yes, yes, yes. I am going crazy here. There is no indication of an outside world. And there is no court case. I mean this country prides itself on civil justice and humanitarianism. How can I just be left to rot in here? Are lawyers so afraid of losing their standing that they refuse to take me on as a client? Where are the human rights organizations? Where is everyone? I asked a cleaning lady—not Ms. Cleaning Lady, she of the notepad, another one—once if anyone says anything about me *out there*, and she shook her head from side to side and smiled, a bright ivory white smile. I wanted to play a tune on her teeth, a tune I played at my first and last piano recital. It was the last one because once I started getting good at playing the piano, I grew bored with the lessons. I think it was "Edelweiss" that I played: I must have been about twelve.

Now, let us imagine my dark brown hair in a high ponytail fastened with a cerulean ribbon. I am wearing a dress—how about a frilly pastel yellow dress?—and ballet flats with dainty white ankle socks with lace. And let us bring to our recollection the teacher, who used to hit me on the knuckles with a wooden ruler during practice. Once she pinched me so hard that I had a bruise on my arm. She begged me not to tell my parents. I never did. Where is she now? Has she read about me in the papers? Does she still teach piano? Does she still hit children?

HOW MANY silent apostates are out there in my country? I remember the story of a local Muslim convert to Christianity who was harassed to return to the faith. When he refused, they threatened to strip him of his citizenship. And yes, in case you are wondering, that person did "return" to the fold of Islam. Was it a true story or fake news? I have no idea. But it is a credible story. I never read about it in the papers, but enough people were talking about it. And we know there is no smoke without a fire.

I want more information about what is going on in the world. I want to know how I am doing out there, the phantom me, the one people must be gossiping about, the one who has sparked controversy and has triggered many debates between liberals and conservatives. All I know is that the paper that published my piece closed down before I came here. Yes, it closed down! Because of my article! It went bankrupt because of the countless lawsuits against the editor-in-chief, coming from neighboring countries as well. One man claimed he was in emotional distress after reading my article. Why would he be if his faith were strong? How frail was his core that an article could shatter it? The editor-in-chief had also been in prison before I was imprisoned. But he came out after two days. There was no court case, but he had a lawyer who argued that the article did not represent his client's ideology and that his client is a devout Muslim and repents for wanting to make sales out of a controversial article. Repents? Was he serious? So he claimed to use me for sales? I doubt the truth of his testimony, the editor is known for his liberal views, but that is a good lawyer and a good argument, I must admit.

Before you jump to conclusions about my country being a totalitarian state, let me say this. In our region, the citizens of my country are considered progressive, and our ruling family is known to be *très* modern. In fact, if the ruling family were making all the legislations in my country, I would not be in jail. And censorship would not even be an issue, unless citizens held views that were threatening to the state, of course. We are considered a semi-democracy, a hybrid government. We have a Parliament, a Ministry Cabinet, and a ruling family. And it was the MPs and their hardline conservative followers who made such a fuss about jailing me.

I am not complaining. I mean, of course, I think it is insane that I am in jail for declaring my apostasy, but I have neither been lashed nor mistreated. I have not been assaulted. Yes, the police were rough when they entered my house, when they pushed me to the ground, when they handcuffed me, but they did not slap me, hit me, punch me, intimidate me with a gun, or beat me with a stick. And we do not have the death penalty here for apostasy as other countries do. So I am not complaining. I am just here because powerful anti-apostate bigots decided to make an example out of me.

I look around at the cell. What is going to happen to me? Am I going to stay here forever? Something has to give, right? I still do not believe my family issued a statement condemning me. They must have been coerced. But where are they? Why are the police so quiet when they come to see me, only asking whether I will sign a paper renouncing apostasy and leaving me alone to my doodles and thoughts? Where is Layla? And Adam. Where is my Adam? I know he scares easily but to not even attempt to see me after all this time?

I am bored. I am restless. My hair smells. It is oily, but what do you expect? I have to be economical with cosmetic products. I do not think we know how much we take our bath products for granted. When I leave here, *if* I leave here, I want to get a Moroccan bath. I feel so filthy. I only wash my hands before meals and take a shower every two or three days, washing or sometimes just wetting my hair once or twice every seven days. And I shower fast. I feel exposed showering in a cell with bars and without plastic curtains, even though whenever policemen want to visit me they send a cleaning lady, sometimes Ms. Cleaning Lady, first to scream *Men! Men!* to warn me of their approach. And ten minutes later, the lady comes back and asks, shouting, whether the police can come in, to which I reply each time without fail: yes. Still, I feel exposed showering, even though the camera is down the hall. What if there is another secret camera somewhere and some perverts are watching me, filming me and sharing the video with their friends? But mostly I shower quickly so as not to waste the bar of soap. About a month ago, when the bar of soap, which was already a sliver, slipped out of my hands and into the squat toilet, I had to wait three doodling days for a replacement.

Alone, dirty, and neglected: I have become an insect, a pariah, an ostracized apostate. This is not the country I believe in. My country is so much better than this. The citizens will not allow this. The world will not allow this. Justice will be restored. Someone will come to my defense. I expect more from the families of this nation and the liberals. Democracy got me in here. How paradoxical is that? I once wrote an article about how I believed we were not ready for democracy, arguing that it is because of the democratic aspect of our hybrid semi-democratic government that we were regressing. I thought I had done the right thing for people who wanted freedom and modernity, but both conservatives *and* liberals bashed me. My argument in the article was more factual than opinionated. I claimed that in the rest of the Arabian Gulf (yes, Persian to the rest of the world, but I am still an Arab), progressive decisions are made with the click of a royal finger, and that is why they are moving rapidly along while we listen to clerics tell us that yoga is a precursor to atheism, concerts should be banned unless the bands sing the national anthem, and women should be covered. Although none of these preposterous propositions are implemented and many people attack the radical mullahs for their restrictive views, including veiled women coming to the defense of unveiled women, some highly connected people make our lives difficult, banning concerts or cancelling events at the eleventh hour, warning people that meditation is *haram*, even closing down a shop selling figurines because the objects could be used for idol-worship. Here, we have to go through the bureaucracy of a legislative body bent on making life hell for locals and foreigners alike. They are bent on curbing our freedoms, bent on trying to segregate women and men, bent on covering up cartoon characters wearing bikinis (The Little Mermaid's outfit was deemed risqué), bent on making it clear that anyone who does not follow Islam is an infidel. Bent, bent, bent. And I wanted straight. Straight. Straight. Straight.

A week later, I wrote an article extolling democracy but expressing my desire that there should be no Parliament for two years until our collective mindset evolved. "No, no, no," they bashed me again. Two weeks later, I relented: democracy wins. I added that it was our mentality that needed to change, and admitted that democracy, as one reader clarified to me, "reflects the majority, and it is selfish to want to eradicate it, albeit transiently, because it does not agree with one's political stance." My sister once said: "Look at America: they have Republicans and Democrats and either side can win, depending on how the masses vote." Okay, okay, I get it. It is selfish that I do not like the Parliament simply because the majority of MPs are opposed to my stance, but maybe one day the tides will change. Yes, democracy wins. Or in the case of my country, semi-democracy wins. I am not a stubborn person—I am quite flexible. Nor do I think my views are the only ones that are right. Mostly, my principles are solid, tucked away in a glass jar, airtight. But I listen, and if another argument is wise, and presented reasonably, I am flexible. I open the jar and let the contents inside breathe. (But not when it comes to apostasy. No wise argument has presented itself as yet.)

AND SO, by writing about apostasy, just rows and rows of words on paper, I committed a crime. By being honest, I committed a crime. And it brought me here to this cell. I was not trying to be controversial. I was not asking for attention. Did I know I would get into trouble? Yes. But when the editor agreed to publish it, I was elated. I thought perhaps some people were ready to read this. Even the editor was not oblivious to the controversy it would cause. Did he warn me? Yes, he did. But he loved the article and was excited to publish it. I recall clearly the words he used: *Brilliant. Outstanding.* There we were, the editor and I, who had not even met, inhabiting an imaginary world. A world where freedom of expression, our mutual raison d'être, swims in our veins, dances in our brains. And in our world it did not matter what others thought at the time, the hoi polloi would catch on, we believed, they had to. Even so, after he agreed to publish the article, I contemplated emailing him to tell him he was crazy for doing so. But I did not. I would not. I could not.

    Had I succumbed to fear, I would be caving into a system, a matrix of hypocrisy and fear mongering. I chose transparency. I chose to be the martyr of penmanship. And here I am. Someone had to do it, and I, a victim of delusions of grandeur, decided that person would be yours truly. I saw myself making headline news: *Dunya Khair makes strides for her country. Dunya Khair, the awakener. Dunya Khair changes antiquated laws. Dunya Khair abolishes the crime of apostasy.*

If I am the first apostate from my country that has come out of the closet, there is a chance for a second, a third, a fourth, a chance for thousands and millions to carry on this work, this legacy. *Dunya Khair, the first apostate paves the way for more!* Being the first gives us hope, being the last is death to a cause. And that is what they want to do, to intimidate me so that no others follow suit, so that no others speak out, so that I am the last of the apostates to come out of the proverbial closet. They tried to brainwash me, but, instead, I washed the brainwashing out of my brain. And I will not be the last apostate to come out. I sense this. I will not live my life inside a closet. No. And nor will others. No.

AND NOW here I am, knees bent, prostrating on the floor.

Now I have become the chorus. I sing: "Oh Beloved. Oh God. Get me out of here. Get me out. I want my family. I want Layla. I want Adam. I want someone to come and get me out of here. I want YOU! Oh God, please!"

For dramatic effect, I pound my fists on the floor. I wail. I pull my hair. There is no sound of footsteps. I am alone. I am all by my lonesome. My hands are sticky with sweat. I crawl on the tiles. In moments like this—well, I have never had moments like this, but I guess this is what happens in such moments—we can easily lose our grasp of reality. My eyelids are heavy. I crawl to the mattress on the floor. I hear footsteps. One of the cleaning ladies, no not *her*, another one, is coming into the cell, carrying a tray of food. She greets me in broken Arabic. I look up at her. I recognize her, but something is different. Ah yes! She is donning a hijab now. She is obviously not a Muslim by birth since I notice that she has a tattoo on her wrist. Tattoos are considered haram although I know many Muslims who have tattoos. I ask if she has converted to Islam and she nods telling me that she bore witness that there is no God but Allah and that Mohammed is the prophet of Allah this very morning. She asks me why I don't pray. I shrug. Ah! She does not know why I am in here. Maybe she thinks I am a drug addict, or I am here for bootlegging, or I have robbed a bank, or I beat up a girl for staring at my husband provocatively. I do not think she would know what apostasy means, although she ought to know: she is an apostate, after all. She left her religion for Islam.

Is it not funny that in my country she can walk freely as an apostate? What do her family and community think of her apostasy? Would her life be under threat there? I want to ask her the next time she comes in, but her Arabic is limited, and I do not want to frighten her. Maybe she has not told her family. Who knows? Or maybe where she is from nobody cares what religion she is. What would it be like to be from a country where I could convert to another religion without the entire country interfering, whether they are for or against my decision? What would it be like to be from a country where apostasy is not frowned upon? Do some societies have thicker skins or are they just more emancipated? What makes one man burn a flag in protest or issue a fatwa when his religion is insulted and another applaud freedom of expression even at the expense of being criticized? What makes people fundamentalists? What makes people so attached to their ideologies that they would kill or go to war in the name of a deity?

If someone is going to insult my views, I will not like him or her much, but I will not want them to be jailed. I would not want to see anyone burn in the afterlife for offending me or anyone else, not that I believe in hell. I would not send them death threats. Nor would I support a petition to have them executed for opposing my belief system. I would simply no longer read their writing (if they happened to be a writer) or unfollow them on social media, and I would pray a silent prayer to bring peace to their hearts, to bring peace to my heart where they are concerned, and to bring peace to all our hearts, addressed to the God I connect with, a divine being who knows how immature we are on the evolutionary scale and who would not use our immaturity against us, just as a human being, from a more elevated level of consciousness, surely would not punish a gazelle for peeing in the open savannah or a lion for killing that gazelle. There is a legal system in place that protects us from pedophiles, rapists, and killers, and I rely on that, I depend on that, not on revenge: that is karma's forte, if karma even exists, and not mine. And if karma does not exist, I have no choice but to accept life's flow.

    Anyway, here I am, crying. Alone in my cell again. The veiled tattooed convert has left me alone with a tray of food. Someone, anyone, come save me. I look at the tray. Macaroni and cheese, a salad of tomatoes and lettuce, a slice of bread, apple juice. I do not feel like eating even though I am hungry. I think I am going to pull a Gandhi and begin fasting. Maybe that will get the police to do something about me. I should have thought of that before. Or maybe I could use my charm and ask one of the maids for a razor? I do not want to kill myself or die: please do not get the wrong idea. I am not feeling suicidal in here, but I want out. It is boring in here, and maybe blood will scare the living daylights out of them. The prospect of death will have my countrymen on edge. And they will take care of me as a result. Citizens count. Of this I am sure.

I HEAR Ms. Cleaning Lady shouting *Men! Men!* I start counting. One, two, three. One hundred. Two hundred. I close my eyes. Minutes pass, the usual. Now she comes back, screaming: *Sister, can the police come now?* To which I reply, *Yes.* Here they are, footsteps approaching. How I love the sound of life, even the sound of policemen. Whenever anyone comes to clean my cell (once a week) or to bring me food (three times a day, pretty spoiled, huh?), I rejoice. Any sign of life is music to me in here. They could bring in an executioner and I would feel less lonely. Today a new chorus has arrived, telling me of an Amiri pardon. The ruler of my beloved country has granted me freedom. What? A pardon is being granted to *me*? Here I was thinking I was forgotten, and I have been on the ruler's mind! It is too much too fast for my mind to register. I ask them to repeat what they just said. And I hear the glorious words again: The Amir has pardoned you. Yes, I heard right.

I ask about my family, but they do not answer. There is too much commotion in the room. Nobody is listening to what anyone else is saying. There are two lawyers standing with four men in black boots. One of the lawyers with a fuzzy beard tells me that my case is an important one around the world. I am tearing up.

There are papers to sign, non-disclosure agreements. I am wary of the one with the beard until he smiles. Phew, it is not a religious beard but a fashion statement. He salutes me for my courage and says he wanted to defend me but was afraid because death threats were sent to his wife and newborn child. How could anyone send a death threat to a newborn? He whispers that he is a big fan of my writing and admires the way I think. Whispering back, I ask him if he is also an apostate, but he dismisses the question, eyes darting across the room. He flushes a deep crimson red, and I have no need for verbal affirmation from him: sometimes the body reveals what the heart conceals. He tells me that I cannot under any circumstances allow the press, local or foreign, to interview me about my time in jail. He says I have become a celebrity. I try to conceal my heart's pleasure, but the corners of my mouth turn upward. If I could dance right now, I would. I ask about my family again, my husband. The lawyer says the world has not forgotten me. It has not? Oh no, it has not! Quite the contrary, I am assured. There have been global protests, social media accounts set up in my name, a viral hashtag: #freedunyakhair, Twitter blasts, countless newspaper articles documenting my imprisonment, and Parliamentary debates. And because of me, some parliament members tried to draft a bill permitting apostasy, but it fell through, sadly. Other MPs tried to push for capital punishment for apostates. This also fell through. Thankfully! I was being used as a pawn by liberals and conservatives, the bearded lawyer informs me, each camp intent on using me to make life a living hell for the other.

And so here I am, signing the NDAs. There are quite a few demands: do not talk about your time in prison, do not write about apostasy, do not speak about your case, do not speak of your interrogation, do not speak of not having had a trial, do not speak of how they raided your house. Interestingly, they have not asked me to sign anything about not writing in general. They have only requested that I stay away from the topic of apostasy and the events surrounding my case.

"Where is my family?" I ask again tentatively. And I add: "Is it true that my family has denounced me publicly?" Finally, after an awkward silence, and a clearing of the throat, a cue I hope entails he is finally going to address the big fat elephant in the room, the bearded lawyer responds: "No, it isn't true. Sometimes, policemen use tactics to get a prisoner to break down. I know it's because they wanted you to renounce your apostasy." The policemen look flustered. They sing: Don't insult our intelligence Beardie! We were only doing our job!

I ask Beardie why my family never visited me. He informs me that they were not allowed to visit, adding: "They love you. I have been in touch with your family every single day since your confinement. Your brother and sister have left the country temporarily, they couldn't handle the publicity. They all love you." Maybe he thinks repeating that they love me will change the subject, but I am not taking the bait. Something is amiss. How can they

WHEN THE HABOOB SINGS

love me if they are not here after the ruler of our country has granted me a pardon? He looks down. My stomach rumbles. Loudly. Loud enough for him to ask if I am hungry. To which I want to reply, only hungry for information about my family. Come on, Beardie.

"Where are my brother and sister?" I ask, tears flowing down my cheek.

"I must respect their privacy." He is biting his nails. This guy knows nothing about concealing his feelings. How can he be a good lawyer?

"Their *privacy*? I'm family, I'm sure they don't mind you telling me where they are."

"They have specifically asked me not to tell you..." He looks around at the other men. They suddenly engross themselves in a separate conversation.

We look at each other, this lawyer and me. It unnerves me that he knows something that I do not about *my* family.

"I don't understand."

He exhales loudly. I notice beads of sweat on his forehead. Oh no, this cannot be good. My stomach rumbles again. I press on it. He bites on his lower lip.

"And my parents?" I ask, guardedly.

"Your mother was admitted to the hospital yesterday."

"What's wrong with her?"

"She isn't feeling well," he says. A cockroach darts across the floor in front of him. He stamps his foot on it.

"Please be more specific," I say, looking down to make sure the cockroach is dead.

"She has low blood pressure." His eye is twitching. Could he be lying? Why is this conversation taking so long?

"Is that all?" Now I am biting my lip.

"Yes," he says, "only low blood pressure. She should be out in a day or two."

"That long for low blood pressure?"

He adds that heart palpitations accompanied her low blood pressure, so the doctors are keeping her under observation. "Anyway," he adds, "you'll see her soon enough yourself. It's time to celebrate. Your case is closed."

"There was no case," I respond, puffing my cheeks out.

"Well, this whole thing can be put to rest," he says. I ask him when the Amiri pardon was publicized.

He tells me it was yesterday.

"So that took a toll on my mother?" I ask. He ignores my question but is staring at me. "And my father?" He looks away from me. I look at each of the men, who look away, avoiding my gaze, now engrossed in another conversation. What is going on?

"Is my father okay?"

I try again: "Is he unwell too?"

Silence.

And I try once more: "Is he dead?"

I am waiting for a response. I ask again. And again. Is he dead? Is my father dead? Finally, I get a nod from Beardie, a nod from the other skinny lawyer, and one nod after another from each of the policemen, and simultaneous nods from all of them. They cannot stop nodding. I want to beg them to stop. They begin singing: *Yes, your father is dead.* I find myself screaming. I look at the bearded lawyer, asking him to confirm it once more, to tell me again. And when he says it, when he says *your father is dead*, when he confirms my father is dead, that my father died of a heart attack, I collapse to the floor. I have not fainted. I just cannot get up. Tears, uncontrollable, flow from my eyes, wetting my face, my cheeks, my mouth. There is a sound coming from my mouth, a composite of blubbering and wailing. It is a guttural, primeval sound. And it permeates the entire cell, spreading its tentacles into the bodies and minds of all those present. I watch the phosphorescent yellow and green sound illuminate their flesh and bones and bubble to the surface of their skin, explode into existence. The sound is watching me now as I rise. But I am not a phoenix. And I am not rising from the ashes. How can I rise when I, myself, am made of ash? How can I rise when I am the dust beneath the soles of shoes? How can I rise when I am the dirt left behind by careless cleaning ladies? Just as I am about to touch the sound, it disappears into the ether. I am shaking as the lawyer, not the fashionable bearded one but the other one, the skinny one, kneels beside me. I hear him say: "May Allah have mercy on his soul." And he hands me a business card with his name: Mishal Amin. What an inopportune moment for an introduction. I begin to laugh. Hysterically. He looks concerned now that I am laughing. Laughing. Bawling. Shaking. Trying to catch my breath. Trying to breathe. Laughing. Bawling. Shaking.

    I am still on the floor when a woman comes into the room. I am no longer the only woman in a cell with six men, four policemen and two lawyers, Beardie and Skinny. The woman, who is dressed in a nurse's outfit— what is a nurse doing here?— is holding a plastic cup in one hand and two pills in the other. I take the cup and drink from it. The water is freezing. I like my water at room temperature. But I am too thirsty to care. Oh, and I never take pills without asking what they are. And even after asking, I still do not take pills. I hate medicine. I have only taken medication when I needed it, in the case of emergencies: like after a wisdom tooth extraction or after an appendix operation, stuff like that. But at this moment, all my reservations are thrown aside. I know they must have known I would not handle the news well and they came prepared. But why did they wait for a woman to bring me the magic pills? One of the lawyers could have administered them to me. Or any of the policemen. I take the pills. I feel chest pain at first. And as the pain subsides, a feeling I can best describe as *I am here, I am aware, I can hear my thoughts, No I am not here, Where is here? Where am I? Ah yes, here...* The tears are still flowing. I feel light-headed, catatonic. I am being led, dragged, outside the cell and down the hall, past the door, into the office. We reach a reception desk. There is a plastic bag. Oh, here are my shoes! I try to put them on, but I cannot. I can barely bend. I need to use the bathroom. Ah, hence the woman! She is here to help me to the bathroom. The men here are not doctors who can touch a woman, so they brought in a lady. How considerate! My bladder is going to explode. I tell the woman I need to pee. The lady takes me inside a bathroom that smells of cigarettes and aftershave, puts me on the toilet seat—I want to squat but I am too sedated to care about hygiene although I do care but who cares?—hands me the hose to wash my private parts, helps me up, and washes my hands for me in the sink. We walk back to the reception desk. Everyone is staring at me. But I do not care. The pills have taken away every ounce of my self-consciousness. *Oh, Baba! Oh, Baba! Why did you die?*

And now the pills become a chorus: "Don't worry, Dunya. This isn't the time to think. Become an empty vessel. Yes, that's right. Roll your eyes. And look: even your tongue is relaxed, dangling outside of your mouth. You know this, but you don't care. You know you are still crying, but the tears are washing away your pain. We got this, even though you don't. Your mom isn't well, your dad isn't coming back. Your brother and sister are far away and don't want you to know where they are. You're alone right now. We got you, sister. We got you. Rely on us."

"What about Adam?" I ask the chorus.

And the chorus sings: "Don't worry about him now. Just relax into this stupor. Yes, that's right. Close those pretty eyes of yours. Don't worry. You have a man holding you on one side and a woman on the other. You're ready to fall, let yourself. Don't be afraid to BLACK OUT. Let go now!"

I LOOK around. I feel lethargic and nauseated. My tongue is dry and the roof of my mouth tastes bitter. I am in a room with white curtains drawn around me, tied to a drip and a monitor, beeping. I am not at all claustrophobic, but I feel an urge to jump out of this bed and scream. I remember being led out of the prison cell. And someone—was it the lady or Skinny?—laying me down on a sofa. I recall vomiting and crying. And I recall Skinny and Beardie holding my hands, telling me an ambulance is on the way and not to worry. Ah yes, the ambulance. Ah okay, now I get it. That is how I got here. And so, here I am. How long have I been here? And yes, of course, I remember that Baba is no longer here, but I feel numb. Have they given me more medication? I want to grieve. I read once that tranquilizers only hit the pause button on pain only for it to come back and haunt you tenfold in time. I want to get the pain out of the way. I want to grieve now. I will have to tell them to stop the medication. But, no, I do not think I would be able to bear it without the pills. Best to stay on them, until I am sure I can deal with things. But I have to recover quickly. I need to be more alert when I meet up with my mother.

Oh no. I am falling asleep again.

THE SOUND of plastic beneath my sheets awakens me. Are they afraid I am going to pee in my bed? I remember waking up several times in the night and ringing the bell for the nurse to take me to the bathroom with my drip on wheels. I have got my bladder under control. But I suppose they are not taking any chances. This time the curtains do not enclose me, and I can see beyond my bed. I count five other beds: two with the curtains drawn and three without. One patient is an elderly woman with false teeth laid out on tissue paper on her bedside table—there is something so disarming about a toothless smile. The second patient looks like a teenager. She does not appear ill at all. The other bed I can see is empty but made up and ready for the next casualty.

    Oh, Baba. Please tell me this is just a dream. Please tell me you are not gone. Maybe they told me you were dead to frighten me, to make me see how grave my actions were. Oh that is impossible. Nobody could be that evil. The lawyers were nice. No, they would never do that to me. Oh Baba, come back. Be alive, Baba. I promise I will not write about apostasy again. In any case, I have signed a non-disclosure agreement, but even without that, I promise I will no longer be controversial. I promise I will never write anything again, just be alive! Be alive, Baba!

The elderly lady props up her pillow. A newspaper falls from the side of her bed to the floor. I want to pick it up for her, but I feel heavy and, as I am stuck to a drip, I cannot move without assistance. A nurse comes rushing to pick up the paper. Wait a minute... That is a photograph of me on the front page: *Dunya Khair released from prison*. I ask the toothless elderly woman if I can borrow her paper. She puts her false teeth back in her mouth, pushing the upper ones back into position with a sucking sound, and says: "You can have it." I want her to hug me, I want her to tell me life gets better in time, but instead I just whisper *thank you*. When I turn toward the nurse and ask her what I am here for, she tells me I had a nervous breakdown. "You will be fine soon," she adds.

The picture of me in the newspaper is embarrassing, cringe-worthy. I am being carried out of the police station. The photographer has captured me at an angle where you can see cameramen and reporters all around me holding gigantic microphones. Oh, I must have been on live television as well. Cringe! I am shamelessly reading about myself. There is a report of the ruler's speech about my case. I wipe away tears as I read that he defends my rights and the rights of all citizens as long as we do not pose a physical threat to the country or his sovereignty. He assures the nation that I do not.

I know that even with all the hate and negativity, I am fortunate to have been born in my country. There are some places where I would have disappeared or been executed or tortured or lashed or left to languish in prison for years and years.

When I reach the part where the ruler of my beloved country proposes that religion be considered a personal matter, I know my purpose on Earth has come full circle. I know the current Parliament will never agree to this, but if the Amir agrees with me, more people may voice their approval of apostasy, and in time, even if it takes a long time, we will have a government in place that no longer interferes with what we believe or disbelieve in. I read on. Human rights activists, most of whom are unsurprisingly women, or men who believe the patriarchy is outdated (including a famous male member of Parliament), are campaigning for the proposal and for amendments to the existing National Unity Law (an ironic name) that considers apostasy as a crime punishable by a period of time not exceeding a year in prison along with a fine. Even though many argue that the law is lenient, in comparison with apostasy laws in other countries, why do we have to go to prison or pay a fine for being apostates in the first place? Does it not say in a verse of the Koran: *There is no compulsion in religion.* And in another verse: *You have your religion, I have mine?*

The penultimate paragraph of the article about me in the paper is disconcerting. A cleric from another country has issued a fatwa against me. And though the article states that our Amir and even MPs in my country have announced the fatwa null and void, his words are menacing, to say the least. The foreign cleric claims that as Muslims, we should not let the West influence us and that all citizens, liberal or conservative, young or old, male or female, must stand united in opposition of my flagrant disregard of Allah and the prophet. But my faith is restored by the last paragraph. There is a statement from a renowned human rights organization about how my beloved country is taking a step in the right direction. I read more details surrounding the Amiri pardon, how our ruler emphasized that this case could be just what we need to make us reconsider our rigid stances, and how we should be unified and not divided when it comes to freedom.

    I always had faith in our ruler, whose main concern is the security and wellbeing of our people. And though I lost faith in Members of Parliament, there is still a part of me that has faith in them, wants to have faith in them at least. What part of me is so naïve as to believe that anyone could be transformed, even a monster? I suppose it was that faith in others, that naivety that landed me in jail. I thought that by declaring my apostasy, I would open the gates of freedom for others and for myself. And perhaps in a minute way I have opened those ironclad gates. Only time will tell. Only time.

THERE IS a flurry of events. The drip is being removed, a doctor is standing before me, tilting his head from left to right. His hand is under his chin now. What is he reading on that clipboard? Does he support me or not? Surely he knows about my situation. Is it going to be like that from now on: me searching for non-verbal, or even verbal, cues to ascertain whether someone applauds or condemns me? There is no in-between with apostasy here unless you are a hypocrite. I remember the lawyer, the smiling one with the trendy beard. There are many more apostates like him lurking around. I feel an obligation to make them all feel safe. Why was my calling not something peaceful and productive and sustaining such as gardening? Why was my calling not something nourishing and palatable such as cooking?

A voice comes out of nowhere: a voice I recognize well. The doctor and nurses turn around to greet the voice.

"Can she leave doctor?" the voice asks. It is Adam. *My* Adam. I knew he would come for me. I say hello to him. He mumbles a quick hello and turns away. I reach for his hand, but instead of clasping my hand in his, he pats my hand and moves closer toward the doctor.

"Yes," the doctor replies, "but we are waiting for the office to send the hospital release form."

"Doctor," I find myself saying, "can I have some more sleeping pills?"

He explains that it is against the law to administer sleeping pills for longer than three days. "To get a prescription, you must go to a psychiatrist. There are many good ones here. I can recommend one for you. Do you feel more comfortable with a male or female?"

"It doesn't matter," I find myself responding. He writes down a few names.

"Here," he says, handing me a piece of paper. I cannot understand his handwriting. I place the paper on the side-table.

"Why do I have to go through a psychiatrist? Why can't you just give me some now?" I ask.

"They are addictive."

"But I'm not addicted. Do I look addicted? Trust me, I'm not addicted. I just need, *want*, I mean *want* the pills. Please. Wait, how long have I been here? I'm not addicted," I say, sounding addicted, to be fair.

"Four days. What you need, I meant *want*," he says, "is rest."

I am taken to the bathroom to change into my clothes. I look at my visage in the mirror. Pale with black circles under my eyes. Sunken cheeks and chapped lips. I notice a cluster of pimples on my left cheek. I touch my forehead. My skin feels scaly. And my hair is plastered to my scalp. No wonder Adam cannot look at me. I scurry out the door.

WHEN THE HABOOB SINGS

Walking down the hall, with a release form in one hand and my husband by my side, we make our way to the parking lot. Adam cannot find the car, but I do not say anything. I know he gets embarrassed when he is lost or cannot find something. We walk to another part of the lot. I hear the beep of his remote. We approach the car.

I break my silence. "Adam, are you okay? You aren't even looking at me."

"Babe, we'll talk when we get home," he says. He turns the key in the ignition.

"How's Mama?" I ask, turning to look at him.

"You have a lot on your plate now, Dunya. I'm sure you want to visit your mom, but I think you need to rest today. We can come back here to visit her tomorrow."

"Wait, Mama is *here*? In *this* hospital?" I turn to face the big, grey building with its blue glass windows. It is the oldest hospital in town, but it has been renovated many times and looks modern now.

He turns the engine off and puts his head on the steering wheel. He shakes his head and tells me we should go home, that he is tired and I must be as well. Oh, but Adam knows me better than that. I open the car door and he grabs me. After releasing myself from his weak grip, I glare at him. He looks down at his feet. I notice his shoes, orange sneakers. And blue shoelaces. Are my powers of observation getting better? Okay, so now you want to know what I am wearing? It is the same outfit I wore months ago on the day of my arrest and the one I wore on the day of my release: a white tunic and faded dark blue jeans with bedroom slippers. (Remember, the police arrested me without warning: I had no time to change into sneakers or espadrilles. Although I hear that people wear bedroom slippers, they call them slides, out of their homes these days—or are bathroom slippers known as slides?—so I guess I am accidentally trendy.) My tunic smells of detergent. I am grateful the hospital staff washed the vomit off. I cannot wait to take a shower.

I get out of the car and slam the door. Adam follows suit.

We are now walking back toward the entrance. I am fidgeting with the tassels dangling from the neck of my tunic. My husband is awfully quiet, but I am sure everything is overwhelming for him, too. Adam leads the way.

Mama has a private room. I walk in. She is sitting on a leather couch near the window, looking at something on her iPad. Adam greets her, kissing her on her forehead, and she smiles at him. I rush to her side. I kiss her on the forehead. I look at her face. Her lips are pursed. "Mom!" I say loudly, as though shouting will remind her that I am her daughter and I am out of prison. Mom looks away and asks me to leave. What? My mother wants me to leave? Is she not excited I am out of prison? What is going on? Does Mom have dementia? Is she not too young for dementia? Which age do people get dementia? Wait... Maybe she *is* angry with me like the policemen said. But the lawyer said the denouncement was fake, a tactic used by police to force me to renounce my apostasy. But maybe the police were telling the truth and the lawyer was lying. Maybe she has denounced me.

My mom tells Adam to get me out of here, but I ignore him when he looks at me, his eyebrows raised, gesturing his head toward the door. Mama walks to the bed and rings the bell for a nurse. Right away, a nurse walks in and my mother tells her to tell me to leave.

"But that's my mom," I tell the nurse.

"She doesn't want to see you. Please respect her wishes and leave her alone."

"Mom, please." Adam and the nurse are holding me, trying to pull me toward the door, and Mom is looking away, screaming: "Get that monster out of here! Get that killer out of here!"

Killer? What on earth is she talking about? Is Mom hallucinating? Something must be wrong with her head. She does not look that ill though. Just tired. And she has lost a bit of weight. Not that much. Not enough to warrant concern.

"Madam, calm down," the nurse tells her.

But my mom is still screaming: "Get her out!" A doctor comes in. He asks us, politely, to leave my mother alone.

My husband becomes the chorus: "Let's leave. I knew this wasn't a good idea."

The doctor joins the chorus: "She is your mother. Don't worry, she will see you soon, but now is not the right time."

The nurse joins in too: "Please, ma'am. Please leave."

I pull away from the nurse. Adam is still holding me. I turn to Mama and say: "I love you, Mom. Please know that." I am sure she does not recognize me. It must be dementia. Poor Mama. She thinks I am a killer.

The doctor is leading Mom to her bed. He covers her with a blanket, lifts a part of it, and injects her with something. She rolls her eyes and passes out.

"Is she okay?" I ask the doctor. He tells me not to worry, that it is a case of nerves, and she will recover soon. I ask if she has dementia.

"Dementia? What? No." The doctor looks confused.

"Is something wrong with her. She doesn't seem to recognize me. What's wrong with her doctor? Is it the medication? Why doesn't she recognize me?"

The doctor is wringing his hands. He looks at Adam. "She just needs rest and—"

"Dunya," Adam says, "let's go home. She knows who you are and she doesn't have dementia."

"So has she publicly denounced me?"

"No Dunya. It's more complicated than that. Let's go home." He takes my hand and leads me to the door. I take one last look at my mother's lifeless frame. We walk out to the hallway. The doctor follows us. I ask him if her blood pressure has been stabilized and if her heart palpitations have stopped.

"Blood pressure? Heart palpitations? Who told you that?" The doctor exhales loudly, looks toward Adam and shrugs.

"Forget it," I respond. I am not in the mood to explain that the lawyer must have lied to me.

We shake hands with the doctor and make our way back to the parking lot. We get in the car. He starts the engine and puts the radio on. I turn it off. He turns it back on again. A song I like is playing.

Pining. Oh darling,
I'm pining for you

WHEN THE HABOOB SINGS

There are leaves to sweep (oh yeah)
And curtains to draw (oh yeah)
Do you yearn, oh lover?
Do you yearn for me too?

As soon as Adam makes his way outside the hospital grounds, I lower the volume on the radio and ask him why he failed to mention that Mama did not want to see me.

"I knew you wouldn't stop nagging until you saw it for yourself, but I didn't want you to see her today. Are you happy now?" His face is red, and he is breathing loudly. I press him for more information, but he tells me he wants to focus on the road and will not say another word until we get home.

WE ARE in our bedroom now. I am laying on our marital bed, fully clothed in my in-prison, out-of-prison, in-the-hospital, out-of-the hospital clothes.

"The lawyer said my family loves me and they ask about me every day. He said the police were lying when they said they want nothing to do with me. But Mom wants nothing to do with me and she seems to have lost her mind. Please tell me what the heck is going on?"

Adam sits beside me on the bed. My eyes are half-closed. I am exhausted, but I will myself to stay awake. I cannot wait another moment to hear what is wrong with my mother even though I am not sure whether I am prepared to hear the truth.

"Don't you just want to take a shower first? Rest a bit? Unwind?"

"Adam, I waited months to take a proper shower, I don't mind waiting a few more minutes."

"Okay. I'll tell you. But are you sure you're emotionally ready to hear this?" His brow is furrowed. He is gritting his teeth. What will he tell me?

"I'm waiting Adam..." I exhale loudly.

"Okay, so here it goes. Your parents privately hired a lawyer the day after you were arrested. The lawyer proposed taking the case to our ruler, to seek an Amiri pardon. Your father and mother kept asking the lawyer to grant them permission to visit you, but the lawyer was too afraid that it would turn into a high-profile case and his identity would be revealed, so he told your parents he would focus only on your release and securing you a pardon. After a couple of weeks of not being able to see you, your dad got restless and went to the jailhouse where you were staying and insisted on seeing you. But the policemen wouldn't let him in without official approval. They said that you were not allowed any visitors. He was heartbroken, and that night he died in his sleep. Your mother blames you for his death." Adam has tears in his eyes.

"He died in his sleep the same night he tried to see me? Oh no! Poor Baba! Oh, my love, Baba! Mama's right to blame me. Oh, I wish you told me all this before I saw her. Why did you stay quiet?"

"I wanted to wait a day or two to tell you. And in any case, you had to see her whether or not she wanted to see you. She's your mother. And I thought if your mother saw you out of jail, she might just change her mind."

"Are you crazy? That's a shock for anyone. She's frail and in the hospital. She had no idea I would walk in. My poor mother! I thought it was going to be a pleasant surprise for her. Oh, I hate myself. Oh, I don't blame her one bit. She's absolutely right to not want to see me. Baba wouldn't have died if it weren't for me."

The room is blurry. All I want to do is sleep and never wake up, or at least wake up in another paradigm where I am not a writer let alone a writer of apostasy. My whole life is now divided into before and after writing the article. I am waiting for Adam to say it is not my fault, but he says nothing. He walks toward the door and leaves the room. How can he just leave me in this state? But he comes back inside our bedroom carrying a cardboard box he places on our bed.

"These are some newspaper clippings, articles, and transcripts of speeches about you. I printed everything significant I could find from the Internet. You're a hero, D. Look, here are speeches from various media outlets and MPs in Great Britain supporting you. Oh, and look at this one. That's the Canadian Prime Minister. Can you believe it? You have to read what he wrote about you. So amazing! Here's an article from an American newspaper. Check this out. Those are American congressmen and women. They love you. Oh, and you're a hero in India too. And in Ghana. Look, here's a clipping from an Australian newspaper. You have fans in New Zealand, Italy, France, Germany. Damn woman! Oh, Belgium, Sweden, Denmark, Norway. Finland. Wait... This one's from South Africa, great article, here's another one from the Philippines. Oh and Botswana, Mozambique. Wow, you have to go through these."

"No Muslim countries? No Arab countries?"

"Only Egypt and Lebanon. Wait let me find the Egyptian one. It's in here somewhere."

"Not now Adam."

He looks at me, puts the cardboard box on the floor. "Yes of course. Take your time. Anyway, I just wanted to let you know you are loved."

"A lot of people hate me."

"Yes, I won't disagree with that. But more people love you. You're a heroine. And even some conservative people are supporting you. You know that famous lady on Twitter, the religious one, Khawla Dua, who always posts about the beauty of Islam? Even she supports you. She is famous and active on Twitter and is using Koranic verses that promote tolerance and forgiveness to defend you. She likes you a lot. Quite a few religious people are defending you. And in some bizarre way, you've brought people together, even if you think you've divided the nation. Some liberals and conservatives are coming together for you."

I want to tell him that is not what the bearded lawyer said when I was being released from jail. He told me that liberals and conservatives are fighting each other using me as a pawn. I want to tell Adam this. Instead, I ask him why he did not pick me up from the police station.

"I was there, Dunya, but I saw all the cameramen and you were out of it. A policeman was carrying you to the ambulance and there were a lot of people outside the station. The media. Fans and protesters. I didn't want to be photographed, so I waited in the car and followed the ambulance to the hospital. You don't remember, but I admitted you to the hospital. You were in and out of sleep."

Wait, I do remember. I remember him sitting on the hospital bed kissing my hand. Yes, Adam was there. My

Adam. I stroke his face. "Thank you," I whisper. I stare at the box on the floor. I do not want to read about myself just now. I need to digest all that has elapsed since leaving prison. I ask Adam about our computers, our cell phones.

Adam tells me they brought all our devices back, but everything has been wiped clean including our contact lists. He got us new chips and new passwords and new numbers. And new laptops registered under false names because he is sure all our old devices would be monitored. But he tells me not to worry: the house is not bugged. He has a friend who is a private detective and he swept our home, finding nothing.

"Do you want your new phone?" he asks.

"Not right now, love. I want a sleeping pill, though. Two pills. And I'm not visiting a psychiatrist. Not now at least. I need a break from everything." I hear him tell me he will make some calls. I want the pills for tonight, I insist. He nods. Yes, I know, I should not consider pills without professional consultation, and I know that I acted all high and mighty stressing that *I only take medicine in emergencies* and so on, but this is a mental crisis and I consider it urgent. I am in so much emotional pain that if you stabbed me right now, I would not care. I would not mind dying, putting an end to this misery. I want to ask him about my brother, about my sister, but I have no energy. All I want to do is sleep. I should take a shower first. My hair is filthy and my body is even filthier. But I cannot move. I close my eyes.

Someone is about to push me off a cliff. And when I turn around to see who is pushing me, it is not my dead father, or my siblings who have run away, or my husband, who seems to be hiding more information from me but who must know it is not the right time to tell me. I look closer to see who is pushing me, half expecting to see my mother. But it is not Mama either. It is me. I am face to face with myself, the self that is about to push me off the cliff. I turn around again and see a cupboard hanging from the cliff, a medicine cabinet dangling from a metal chain. If I can just manage to reach it, I may just save myself from being pushed by myself into the abyss. I look down. There is a stream, a waterfall, and a verdant roof of trees. It will hurt if I fall. And though I am terrified to jump, the pain of falling is better than the pain that awaits me if I do not fall. When I look up again, the medicine cabinet has disappeared. I wake up drenched in sweat, alone.

    I am ready to take a shower. I close the bathroom door, undress, and step into the shower. The warm water caresses my body. I pour shampoo onto my palms and massage my scalp with my fingers. Oh, how I missed the smell of shampoo. After rinsing my hair, I apply conditioner and scrub my body with a loofah and exfoliating body wash to rub off all the dead skin on my arms, my legs, my breasts, my stomach, my back, my buttocks, my feet. The drain hole is clogged with dead skin and strands of hair. Jenny will clean it. I need that Moroccan bath soon.

    Adam knocks on the door. *Come in!* I shout. He opens the door but does not come in, speaking to me from behind the door like a stranger, informing me that he is going out to meet a friend. *Now?* I ask. He says his friend has a box of sedatives. I ask him not to take long, that I don't want to be alone. He promises he won't take longer than half an hour.

I am still surprised the hospital did not give me a farewell gift of pills. Surely, the threat of a nervous breakdown trumps the risk of addiction.

ADAM RETURNS home in twenty-three minutes (but who's counting) with a box of pills. I do not want to take them. But I will keep them as a security blanket. I am sure I will need them soon, but not right now. I am alone in my thoughts. There is no chorus taunting me, no part of me threatening myself. There is just silence. And though I welcome the silence, it is eerie, kind of like the calm before a storm. I hope no storm awaits me, but if it does, I have the shelter of these little pills. Sleep is overtaking me. I put the box in the first drawer of the bedside table. All I want to do now is drift off to...

IT HAS been two weeks since my release. I went back to the hospital two days after the first time I saw my mother, but she had been discharged. I drove to my parents' house that day, the house I was raised in, which held the ghost of my father and will now be known as Mama's place. Hands trembling, a feeling of dizziness engulfed me on the way there. I grasped the steering wheel, shook my head, patted my cheeks at a traffic light to keep myself from falling asleep. No, I had not taken the pills. I was just exhausted. I pulled over to the side of the street at one point. A patrol car officer parked in front of me about fifteen minutes later to find me bawling with my head on the steering wheel. He tapped on the window. I ignored him, thinking he might go away if I pretended he was not there. But he would not stop tapping.

"Yes," I said, rolling down the window.

"Are you okay?" His breath reeked of nicotine.

"Yes," I responded, trying but failing to stifle further inhalation.

"Hey, aren't you that lady—"

I could tell from his tone he was not a fan, so I rolled up the window. He snarled at me, and I heard the word infidel. I glared at him through the glass, but not one to be intimidated, he glared back, pointing his index finger at me as he walked away, his boots making a squeaky sound as they scuffed the gravel. I started the engine and made my way to Mama's. I rang the bell. The maid, my nanny Alice, who had raised me, opened the door.

"She doesn't want to see you," she whispered, closing the door slowly.

"Alice, please let me in," I begged, pushing the door. She relented, and I walked with her down the long corridor. The walls are covered with paintings on both sides, as my father was an avid art collector. I have no eye for art. Sometimes, to support the local art scene, I will buy art, but I always give it away. But my parents were always obsessed with art, taking us to galleries across the globe and even to a couple of auctions. So our house is a museum. Guests were always staring at the artwork on the walls. Some of them are pricey, more than pricey, extremely pricey, the kind of art that should be locked away when people are around. But we live in a safe country. Nobody has ever stolen any of our paintings. But, in my humble opinion, our piece de resistance is in our reception room: a J.C. Verdier La Platine Magnum turntable that weighs around four hundred kilograms. You do not want to know how much it costs, believe me. And yes, it works.

I entered the living room, with Alice trailing behind me, one of four living rooms in my stately childhood and adulthood home, and there she was, my beautiful Mama, sitting serenely, reading a magazine. She saw me, hurled the magazine across the floor, and turned toward Alice, giving her the kind of look a wife would give a husband who walked in with a mistress.

"Get out, you infidel! Get out, you killer! I curse you. Leave my sight! If you ever enter this home again, I will call the police," she hissed. She turned to Alice and threatened never to talk to her if she ever let *the infidel* inside the house again. Alice began crying and scurried out of the living room.

Every night since seeing Mama that day, I have cried myself to sleep. Adam is withdrawn and aloof. He leaves for work without saying goodbye and we eat our meals mostly in silence without even looking at each other. And for the last few nights, he has slept on the couch. When I asked him why the night before, he said my sobbing keeps him up and he needs to be fresh for work. Oh! I cry even *while* I am asleep. There is only so much a body or a mind can take, I suppose. And so I thank my body for doing its work.

I still have not taken the sedatives, even after my awful encounter with Mama, but I have a feeling I will need them soon. I am tired again. This time, I do not cry, I howl myself to sleep, a sorry excuse for a lullaby. But I cannot sleep. Thoughts are racing in my head. I scramble to focus on each of them. One thought tells me I am a victim, another tells me I am a perpetrator. One thought tells me my family should be ashamed of themselves for abandoning me, another tells me I deserve everything that has happened to me. This latter thought gets louder and louder until I accept it as the truth. *I brought this on myself. I wrote the article.* What did I expect? Handshakes and hugs? Awards and accolades?

I am now officially scared. "Adam! Adam!"

He rushes into our room and sits beside me on the marital bed, holding me, hugging me, and promising me that time is a healer. "Please lie down next to me," I tell him. He is shaking and his eyes are bloodshot. I ask him what is wrong. He lets go of me abruptly and stands up and paces the floor beside me.

"Adam, please. What is wrong with you, my love? Tell me."

"I can't do this. I have become a pariah at work. I can't be with you anymore."

I notice how much weight he has lost. Why did I just notice this? Is something wrong with me? He tells me again that he wants to leave me. How can he come rushing in, hug me, hold me, and now tell me he wants to leave? He repeats over and over again: I can't do this. I can't. I can't.

"You can't do this? What about *me*?"

"D, I can't. I just can't—" He is leaning against the wall across from the bed, our bed, our marital bed.

"Adam, look at me! My father is dead. *Dead!* My mother won't talk to me. I have been trying to call my brother and sister for weeks now as you know. They both won't answer me. I know that they have both read the messages I sent them. Oh, and I didn't tell you, but I finally checked my email. I have so many death threats. And my phone rings non-stop. I have to keep it on silent throughout the day. I can't answer most of the calls because I'm terrified they are the press or human rights organizations, and I don't want to go back on the NDAs.

Oh, Adam. You can't leave me now." I get up from the bed and walk toward him. I am holding his arms, stroking his arm hair. I can feel his hairs standing on end.

"This is too much. Your views are too much right now." He pulls away from me gently.

"*My* views? Coming from an atheist? How can apostasy be too much for *you*? I believe in God. *Your* views are more scandalous than mine. Is my honesty too much for you? Is that it? Is there another reason? Is there someone else?"

"Are you out of your mind? Someone else? You've lost it, D. I'm not that kind of a man. I just can't handle this. I want a normal life. People are wary of me. I miss our life before all this happened."

"Why can't you just applaud me? If you had announced your atheism, I would not just hold your hand in public, I would parade you in front of the world."

"Oh, so you're trying to make me feel guilty?" I watch him pace the room some more, this time wringing his hands.

"I'm not trying to make you feel anything. I want you to know that's what love is."

"Let's not pretend this is some grand love story, D. It was an arranged marriage." He looks at me, wild-eyed, panting for breath. His hair is not brushed, and he looks disheveled, his shirt and pants wrinkled. Is he losing his grip on reality, too?

"Arranged or not, I love being with you. To me, this is love. It doesn't matter how it happened."

"You don't understand..." He sits down on the floor, cross-legged. I sit down, facing him, with my knees bent.

I take his hands in mine. He finally looks me in the eyes, with tears streaming down his face.

"Well help me understand. I'm your wife. And I'm a wreck. I need you. I'll die if you leave."

"Please don't say that. You're a tough cookie, D," he says, between sobs. "You defied our society, survived a couple of months in jail. I'm sure a break will be good for both of us. I'm not talking about a divorce, that's the last thing on my mind. I'm just asking for a brief separation to get myself back together. I just—"

"We can piece each other back together again. I can't do this alone, Adam. Look, I know you've always cared about what others think. I know your two faces, the public and the private one, but when the shit hit the fan, you were there for me. You fought for me on Twitter. We adore each other baby even if it's not a grand love story. We can make it through this. You should be supporting me more than anyone else, not just because you're my husband, but because you are a victim of this system too. You can't even announce your atheism publicly. We should be fighting this battle together. But you want to leave me when I need you the most?" I look at him, hopefully, searching for a sign that my words have had some effect on him. Nothing.

"You signed NDAs. We can't fight this. You know that."

"Regardless of what I can do publicly, you should be here for me privately. Fight for me here in our home. Fight for me by fighting any part of you that wants to leave me. Get through whatever is going on inside you. For me. For us. I need you so much. Don't leave me."

"I'm not leaving you. I'm just asking for a break. And it's not your views. You know I support them. Come on, D. Don't twist things."

"I'm not twisting things. You are the one who said my views are too much for you."

"Well, I didn't mean it like that. It's the fact that you publicized something personal. You put our lives at risk. I get death threats every week." We are still holding hands, miraculously. Even amid this tension. He is rubbing my hands with his. That is a good sign, right? He kisses my cheek. Another sign. Okay, so this cannot be that bad.

"So do I. That's not going to change how I feel about you. I swear I'll hit rock bottom if you leave me now. Please wait until things settle down at least. I beg you. We could leave the country until things wind down." He pulls away from me and stands up. I get up, too. I touch his face, but he turns his head away. "Stop," he says. "Leave me alone. I've made up my mind."

And this time a different kind of chorus appears: it is an elephant, *the* elephant, the one in the room that we are trying, but failing, to address. A big elephant in a pink tutu sings: "He doesn't want to be with you. It's too much of a risk. It's over. It's over. You shouldn't have written the article. Stop looking for signs. He is conflicted, but it's over. Go back to religion, you sinner, you infidel."

A silent chorus inside my head responds: "He's an atheist. What would going back to my religion do? It wouldn't bring him back to me. He's not leaving because of my views. He's leaving because of society. He prefers the haven of hypocrisy to true freedom and authenticity."

And the elephant chants: "Well, that says something about you. Judging him for being a hypocrite, but you're the hypocrite, wanting to stay in a relationship that is confining and inauthentic."

"You don't know him the way I do," I sing to the chorus, and in my reverie, my voice is breaking, my lips are quivering.

"I, the omniscient elephant in the room, know him better," says the callous behemoth. And now it is dancing the dance of victory on tiptoes. "Oh yeah! Oh yeah!" it chants. Could this be a new kind of lyric poem, an epode of sorts?

"They beat me up, Dunya," Adam says, bringing me back to the moment, our cliff-hanging moment, the moment from which our future dangles. Though a separation is not a divorce, I still feel a part of me dying. I do not want to be alone. I want Adam. I look at my husband. He looks back at me, challenging me to look away. I do. His eyes are defiant.

"Who?"

"Some random guys in the parking lot of my office. I was working late and there were two of them. I went to the hospital. They took a bunch of X-rays and a scan. Nothing was broken, but I had bruises everywhere." He is crying again.

"I'm so sorry!" I wail. "I'm so sorry!" I try to touch him, but he recoils. My husband, who has let me touch him for more than two years, is now in the habit of recoiling from *me*, his wife.

"Remember when we secretly agreed during our engagement not to have children? I knew you were the one for me then. I knew it. I thought, where could I find a woman who doesn't want kids? And even all this that you're going through. Don't think for one second that I don't admire you. You're amazing. You're strong, you're courageous, and you're iconic. I envy your bravery, but I'm not cut out for this. *You* are. I've always been happy living in the shadows. I don't want to play with fire. You're fine with all that. It's as if you want to be in the fire." He wipes tears from his eyes and scratches the nape of his neck. I have the instinct to kiss his forehead but am afraid of rejection. How did we reach a point where I am certain my husband will reject me?

"I need you now more than ever. All that matters to me is you and finding a way to make peace with my family, especially my mother." My hands are trembling, shaking uncontrollably.

"Dunya, she's your mother. She'll come around. She's grieving. She needs to be angry with someone. I know you don't believe me, but it's not your fault. Your dad was a chain smoker, he never exercised, and he was always stressed out. He was a ticking time bomb. He was always working late. He had so much money but was always at work. He hardly ever took vacations. He could have afforded to slow down ages ago when he sold your grandfather's tanker business, but he just kept stressing himself out more, biting off more than he could chew. He owns enough of the real estate in this country to feed an entire village, but he always wanted more. His death has nothing to do with you. Any stressful situation could've killed him." Adam sits down on the sofa. I am not going to sit beside him. He is pouting with his arms crossed around his chest. I want to hug him, to hold him, but I am tired and wary. I am not going near him. He has made it clear to me that he needs space.

Look at me, I want to say. *Look at me while you're speaking to me. I need you more than ever,* I want to say to him again and again and again. *Don't let me down now. Not now. Please baby.*

"I appreciate you thinking that, Adam, I do. But he died because of me. And now you're going to leave me, and *I'm* going to die."

"Stop saying that." He sniffs loudly. His breathing is still labored.

"Do you care for me?" I look at him, shyly, scratching the cuticles of my index fingers. I started doing this when I was a kid. It is an odd habit, but when I get nervous, agitated, or self-conscious, which is often because I am shy, I still do it. And if I am extra nervous, I pick at my cuticles. If you take a look at my fingers, they are red around my nail area. I do not bite them off as I have seen others do, but the damage is just as bad. Sometimes I have to wear Band-Aids.

"Yes, I do. What a stupid question, D. But I care about my life and my sanity. And I can't continue to live with this fear, *in* this fear. Every day, I feel like vigilantes are going to burst in and shoot us."

"Vigilantes? Adam. Listen to yourself. You're getting paranoid. That's what they want. They want us to be afraid so that we conform."

"We have to conform. You saw what happened when you didn't. Do you want us to go through that hell again?" Adam is pacing the room again. I wish he would calm down. He is scaring me. Are we in danger?

"I'm out of prison now, and I can keep a low profile for a bit. But I can't forget my mission." My heart is beating fast.

"What do you mean your mission? What are you planning next? Oh no, D. You can't do this to us again." He scratches his forehead and glares at me. I see him blinking furiously, uncontrollably. Is Adam going mad?

"Don't you dream of a future where apostates are no longer persecuted? Wouldn't that make you happy? A society where even atheists like you would no longer feel ashamed or afraid? I'm not saying it will happen in our lifetime, but freedom of belief is being discussed for the first time in our country's history. And we have a wise humanitarian ruler. If it were in his hands, he would change this. It's just the Parliament blocking the way now, but times will change. I know it. I have galvanized enough people to carry on with this. But maybe I can do something. Maybe I can find a way around the NDAs. There must be a way. I'm figuring it out. I can't just stop because they want me to." My stomach rumbles loudly. I feel an urge to rush to the bathroom but resolving this with my husband is more urgent. I hold myself, but the rumbling gets louder until even Adam looks at my stomach. I state the obvious and tell him it is my stomach. Somehow, that makes me feel less self-conscious. And I tell myself: I don't need to use the bathroom, just yet. Nerves. Just nerves. Like Mama.

"You need to calm down, D. You're rambling. Forget about saving our country from itself. Just relax. I beg you. Just try and get your life back. Later, you can figure out what to do. And forget about this mission of yours. Just focus on getting your life back, D." He presses his lips together and scratches his moustache.

"It's not *my* life, Adam. It's *our* life. You're my life. My family is my life. How can I get any semblance of my life back when you guys want to have nothing to do with me? You guys are my priority. But I need your love and support." I want to add that I can forget about my mission, but do I have a choice? Even if I never write another article for the rest of my life, I cannot forget my mission. It is in my bones, written on scrolls before I was even a fetus in my blessed mother's womb. Even when we try to forget, our mission finds us. And when we ignore it, we suffer. But I am not concerned with that right now. I want Adam to stay with me. Here in our home.

"Oh, D, I love you. And I support you. I don't know what to do. I don't want to go, but I can't stay here either. Please respect my need for space."

My husband's brain reminds me of a sputtering engine: it is never sure whether to stop or start, to move forward or regress, so it is constantly oscillating between indecision and surety. His mind has been swinging on a pendulum between supporting me and distancing himself from me ever since I wrote the article. And more recently, he seems afraid of me. Perhaps it is because he sees me as his mirror. Maybe he is scared that by looking at me, by staying beside me, he will be infected with authenticity and will end up declaring his atheism to the public, only to suffer my fate and worse. Honesty is contagious. Standing up for oneself is contagious. And that is why they want to inoculate us against being true to ourselves, so that we pay homage only to their way, however absurd, however insulting pledging allegiance to the collective is to the individual soul. Why does fear win again and again? It has invaded my society, my life, my marriage, and even my own mind. I know this now. I have no defense mechanisms in place, no armor to protect myself. Both my outer and inner soldiers have abandoned me.

"I do respect your need for space. Nobody can respect you the way I do. I respect everyone, but it seems like nobody respects me. You are all taking out your grief and frustrations on me. That's selfish."

"It's selfish that you don't understand how you have put all our lives in danger."

"I'm sorry, Adam. I am so sorry baby. You must know that. But someone had to do this. How much longer will we keep up this façade in our society? There's too much fear. It's not normal. I spoke on behalf of everyone. Is that considered selfish to you? Go ahead and think that. I can't change your mind. But please consider that I put my life in danger too. How selfish is that? Oh, Adam, let's move on from this. Please, baby. Let's change the subject for now. Please don't leave. Look, I'm too fragile to have this discussion. And if you insist on leaving, at least don't leave me now. Let me regain my strength. If you've made up your mind, I won't stop you, but please hang in there for my sake. At least for a year."

"A year!" He coughs uncontrollably. I see veins protrude from his neck and his face turns crimson red. His body is clearly rejecting everything I say. He catches his breath and whispers, "No way. That's too long. Way too long."

"Too long? We made a lifetime commitment, and a year is too long for you now? You hate being with me that much?"

The chorus interrupts me: "He can't handle it. He can't. Set him free, apostate. The whole world is against you, and the ones who are not against you can't approach you for fear of alienating society. Take the pills, infidel. Take all of them. One by one. You deserve to die."

I contemplate taking the pills. But conditioning brushes that thought aside for now, occupying the space in my mind. Conditioning is a beast, a demon that creeps up on you when you least expect it. Just when you think your mind has expanded, it taunts you, haunts you, reminds you of all the spooky stories you heard as a child about a vindictive deity and a fiery afterlife for those who leave the faith. And it is because of this conditioning that I now, in a state of religious relapse, am questioning whether I am being punished for writing about apostasy. Is God condemning me for leaving Islam? Has God caused my family and husband to be repelled by me?

I did not go all the way to jail only for my conditioning to take hold of me—but I am too weak to fight it right now. I pound my fists on my chest, slap my cheeks, and pick at my cuticles. I fall on my knees. Adam faces me, with tears in his eyes. Now he is facing me, kneeling, and holding my face in his hands. I tell him I need him to be calm, to soothe me. And he nods. I push him away and punch myself in the stomach but he grips my hands. His eyes and face betray a sense of underlying panic. My face is wet with tears and disillusionment. He is still holding my hands down and is now kissing me all over my face. Is this what will make him stay? The threat of my collapse? I am wailing now, and he embraces me. What is wrong with him? I hear him promise me he will stay but insists that we should move.

"To another country?" I ask in between sobs.

"No, to a new neighborhood. You and me. I won't leave you, D. I'm sorry. This is too much. I wasn't thinking straight. Please forgive me. Let's just move and not tell anyone where we're going."

"But Mama—" I say, gasping for breath.

"She will call me if she wants to reach out. I'll find us a place tomorrow."

"Good idea," I lie. I do not have the strength to say anything else. And I do not want to ruin the moment. I feel numb. If death comes to me now, I will not resist it.

I sit down on the floor, and hug my knees, rocking myself back and forth, back and forth, back and forth. I cannot control the tears. I think of my father, and his appreciation for literature, and I wish he were here, holding me, reading a book aloud to me. If he were here, my mother would be beside me, too. My brother, Yasser, and sister, Alia, would be here, and we would be rejoicing at my freedom. Adam carries me to the bed. He sits beside me caressing my hair. We are both crying to the beat of the chorus.

The chorus is singing, telling me I was killed in prison and this is the afterlife. It tells me I am in a hell of my own making. The chorus keeps singing, but my voice is louder than the chorus now: "Come back, Baba! Come back! I will never write again! I promise! I will cut off these hands, cut off these wrists for you. Come back! Damn expression! Damn freedom! All I want is you: the breathing, living you. Was it worth it? No! Even if my country passes a law, a miracle of miracles if I live to witness it, I choose you over all that, Baba. Oh, Baba! Come back!"

I do not want to move to another neighborhood. But I cannot tell Adam that. He is scared for his life and is worried too many people know our address here. I want to stay here, stitched onto the Persian carpet gifted to us by Adam's mother. (Yes, even Arabs agree it is Persian when it comes to rugs.) I want to become an inanimate object with no feelings, no knowledge of existence. I want to disappear into nothingness. I want to be nothingness with no "I" to know it. But I repeat to Adam over and over: "Yes, a new place. Yes, look for it tomorrow. Yes, you and me." I am not sure he loves me anymore, I am not sure he ever did. But I love him, and I will do anything to make him stay. I will go where I do not want to go just to be with him.

But the chorus tells me I don't love him; I *need* him. "Even your love is selfish," it says. "You just don't want to be alone. If you loved him, you never would've put him into this mess."

I argue with the chorus, defending my love for Adam.

"You're not even compatible," the chorus sings. "He's too weak for you. Your mission is to awaken your country, and he will hold you back. You need a man who supports you, dresses you for battle, and holds the fort. You thought that by marrying Adam you would be riding the same wave into eternity together, but when the boat started rocking, he began swimming toward the shore, alone. He only changed his mind about leaving because your breakdown scared him. Once you stop crying, he'll leave again."

I look at Adam. Will our marriage survive this? But I suddenly do not care. I am too tired to care about him, the chorus, Mama, Yasser, Alia. All I care about now is going to sleep. I cannot even be bothered anymore. This conversation has been draining. Everything is draining. Adam has come face to face with my fragility, but he still does not know the recesses of my mind, he cannot see the walls caving in and engulfing me. He cannot see the fierce battle I am fighting inside myself. No, all he cares about is himself and how this is affecting *him*. He wants a break—*a break*?

Why is he turning all of this into a marital issue? This whole thing is between society and me, the government vs. me, myself, and I. Yes, it has affected everyone around me, but that is what revolutionary ideas do. And now, even amid this exhaustion, amid all the turmoil and uncertainty, I am proud of being a revolutionary.

I feel my body sinking into the bed. My husband is holding me now. "Will you sleep beside me?" I ask, tentatively. His face speaks to me, a silent chorus that relays to me the word *No*.

It does not matter right now. I am too tired to argue, to beg him to hold me and caress my hair until I fall asleep. I will sleep alone again, without Adam, without pills. Maybe I *am* stronger than I know. Yes, I have broken down and collapsed, but who would not after what I have been through? My husband is ambivalent toward me, my siblings do not care whether I live or die, some people in my country want me dead, and my mother—someone who is supposed to love me unconditionally—hates me. Yes, I have the right to break down.

Still, I must be stronger than I know. I mean, I collapse into bed every evening from exhaustion and a sense of dread and still wake up in the morning ready for a new day, and I manage to sleep every night without someone to sing me a lullaby or pills to knock me out. That is strength, is it not? However, after all I have been through, the idea that my husband wanted a break from me might just be the straw that will break the camel's back. Separation, though, is not a straw: it is a heavy trunk filled with weighty objects. Separation may not just break the camel's back, it might kill the camel. But surely Adam will not leave. He compromised by asking us to move. Will he change his mind in the morning? Will he change his mind again when we move to a new place? Will he bring up a separation again? I saw the repulsion in his eyes when I asked him to sleep beside me. I know he brought up moving to pacify me. So is he waiting until I am in a better state to tell me he wants to leave again? I am holding onto my husband with the flimsiest of twine. What I need, though, is the security of a thick rope. Only a thick rope can save our marriage.

Oh, I do not know. What matters is that, for now, I have Adam. And I will hold on to him. This is my personal mission: to regain Adam's commitment and my family's love. I will get them back, one by one. I remember the policemen taunting me, saying that my family did not want me and that my husband would divorce me. They thought they were lying to me earlier, but their words now ring true. Go figure!

The lethargy is stronger than ever. Adam kisses my forehead and tells me to go to sleep. I watch as he turns off the light and closes the door behind him. It is dark and cold, exactly how I like it. This exhaustion is a blessing. I do not need the pills, I tell myself. *I am strong*, I say to myself. *I am strong*, I repeat, trying to convince myself. *I am str—*

I WAKE up. Alone in my marital bed once again. I remember sleeping at my cousin's house when I was younger and telling Mama that Aunty and Uncle slept in separate rooms. She told me never to mention it again, as though it were an anomaly, something too strange and wayward to speak of aloud. But now, faced with the same situation, I presume that many couples must be sleeping separately, keeping up appearances while their marriages hang by a thread. In my case, I am living with a husband who wants to leave but feels guilty. And if guilt will make him stay, I will keep inducing it in him until the thought of leaving or taking a break vanishes from his mind, never to return and plague our marriage again.

It is six in the morning. I walk to the bathroom. Taking a shower has become the highlight of my day. It is the only space where I feel in control. I can decide whether I want to wash my hair or not. I get to regulate the temperature of the water. I can choose to scrub my body with an exfoliator or lather myself with creamy soap liquid. And after the conditions I endured in prison, I do not take luxury products for granted anymore. Scouring the supermarket aisles for new bath products has become my indulgence.

I want to stay in the shower, but the soap is stinging my cuticles, and I remember that Adam has to wake up soon for work, so I rinse my body quickly. It is steamy when I come out. I wrap my silky wet hair in a towel. Damn my hair smells good. Jojoba and guava, according to the shampoo bottle. I wipe the mirror with my palm and face myself, naked in my towel turban. I write the word "help" in lowercase letters on the mirror. I add an exclamation mark. I write it again, and again: this time in capital letters, this time with more than one exclamation mark. I wipe the mirror clean with a hand towel, but I still see the word written faintly all over it. I slather lotion over my arms and legs and wrap myself in a bathrobe. After changing into a house caftan, I open the door and walk to the living room. There is a blanket folded neatly on the couch with a pillow perched above it. Where is Adam? Did he even sleep here last night? I check the time. It is 6:20 a.m. Jenny, the maid, will be awake by now. I dial 104. She answers the phone.

"Yes, madam."

"Where's Adam?" I suck the cuticle of my right index finger.

"Sir is out."

"When did he leave?" Oh, it is bleeding more.

"Last night, madam, after dinner. You want coffee, madam?"

"No, thanks," I say. "Can you get me Fucidin cream and Band-Aids please?"

WHEN THE HABOOB SINGS

"Yes, madam."

I dial Adam's number. He does not respond. I try again. And again. Nothing. I leave a message. I am tired again now. I remove the towel from my hair and sit at the dressing table. I plug in the hairdryer and dry my hair with my fingers and a diffuser. I apply face cream. I feel my eyelids getting heavy. I walk to the bathroom, remove my caftan, and slip into pajamas. I get back into bed and slide under the covers. I do not have to sleep, but I can rest, I can lie down a little. Or maybe I can take a short nap. At least that way time will pass, and I do not have to sit here waiting for Adam to call or come back home. I hear knocking at the door. Who is it? It is me, Madam. Come in, Jenny. She walks in with the cream and a box of Band-Aids. I am too tired to sit up. She takes my hand in her hand and applies the cream to my index finger and then covers it with a Band-Aid. I hope she washed her hands first. I should have asked her before. My eyes are closing. I tell Jenny to turn the lights off.

I am walking inside a tunnel. Is this what they call lucid dreaming? I know I am in a dream. So can I control this? Lights changing color, flashing lights. Pink, yellow, blue, electric yellow, orange, even purple. I see Adam at the end of the tunnel, but he cannot see me. "Adam! Adam!" I shout. "Adaaaaaaaaaaaaam!" I know I am asleep, but this cannot be a lucid dream if I have no control, right? It is a partial lucid dream, the chorus informs me. "Wake up," I urge myself. I push up as though I could will myself to arise from this nightmare by sitting up straight. Someone is whispering loudly. It sounds like Baba. *Harder, Dunya.*

Push harder. But my eyes are shut tight. I try to squeeze them open. It is of no use. "Adam! Help!"

"Madam, wake up. Oh, Madam!" I look up. It is Jenny. I jolt up.

I am panting. It takes me a few moments to recover my breath. I am drenched in sweat. Jenny is rubbing my back and looking at me, aghast. "Madam, you were shouting. Sorry, I came inside without knocking." Adam has told Jenny that she should never, under any circumstance, enter our room unless Adam and I were both out. *Unless it's an emergency,* he added. I suppose Adam never anticipated this kind of emergency, where I am shouting in a partial lucid dream. Yes, this constitutes an emergency. For both Jenny and me.

I hold Jenny's hand to reassure her. She lets go of my hand and walks toward the bathroom. She comes back with a wet hand towel and rubs it across my forehead. "Lord have mercy," she whispers. "Lord have mercy." I know Jenny is a devout Christian. She once told me a man in the supermarket here tried to convert her, and when she said she did not want to become a Muslim, he told her he would pray for her. I remember my brother once telling me when we were kids that he wished he were a Christian. When I asked why, he explained that Christianity is all about love and forgiveness, and Christians sing at church, and their funerals are so elegant. But I think it was mostly because he wished he were a blond and blue-eyed Englishman, a proper white Anglo-Saxon Protestant. My brother has always been in love with everything English.

Just as the chorus in my head begins to sing "Praise the Lord," I am jolted back to the moment by Jenny's repeating: "Madam? Madam?"

"Is Adam back?" I ask nonchalantly.

Jenny shakes her head. She has got that worried look on her face, the kind that makes me freak out. "I'm sorry for coming in, Madam. I was scared. I thought something happened to you."

"It's okay, Jenny. Oh, Jenny." I pull her close to me. She hugs me and I cry in her arms. She cries along with me.

Here we are, two people crying in a room. I am crying because of the new world I inhabit, and she is crying in empathy. But maybe her tears are long overdue. Who knows what stories haunt Jenny? Is it the distance from her family that is making her cry now, or is it really me she is crying for? Has someone broken her heart too? What drives her to cry today? Her tears cannot be flowing just for me. There are tears in all of us, mostly suppressed, tears from being trained to say *I am fine* when someone asks how we are. Nobody wants to hear what we are going through. Our own families cannot handle our stress. But our tears push through, sometimes coming out when we least expect it, to clear and to alleviate our traumas.

We each have internal landscapes and climates. Torrential rains have been plaguing my aura lately: there have been floods and even a tsunami warning. I am on high alert. But how do I escape from myself? There is nowhere to hide from the waves surging inside me. There is nowhere to turn from the rising sea levels. What will I do when the sirens blare? Will I drown? Or will the storm pass and leave me unscathed?

    I tell Jenny I want to take another nap. She leaves the room. I fall asleep and wake up to the sound of my cell phone ringing. I am about to pick it up but the ringing stops. I check the screen. I have a missed call from Adam. I look at the screen again. It is four p.m. now. Adam is calling again. I pick it up this time. I hear his voice, but I cannot understand a word he is saying. It is too loud inside of myself. After he stops talking, I hear him say, "Dunya, Dunya," but I cannot speak. I hang up the phone, stunned by my inability to say a word, and turn my cell phone off.

    The chorus translates to me what has just transpired: "He is not coming back. He wants to look for a new apartment for himself, alone, because he cannot be with you. He will not divorce you. It's just a separation. He wanted to give you both some more time to acclimate to everything, but he cannot deal with this any longer. He will not move out just yet, but he would rather not talk when he gets home. And no, Dunya, he knows what you are thinking. But, no! He was not with a woman last night, he swears, but do you believe him? He passed out at his mother's house, his mother who has not spoken to you since you left the prison cell, but who has told him it is best to stay with you since it's his duty as a husband, and since nobody in their family has ever gotten a divorce. His mother insisted it would be a shame to break the record, even in the exceptional and unfortunate case of being married to an infidel."

WHEN THE HABOOB SINGS

The chorus abruptly stops. I cannot believe his mother has not even called to check on me or pass a message to me through Adam. I know she is a religious woman, so religious that Adam cannot confess his atheism to her, so religious that she is embarrassed and dismayed by my apostasy, but she has carried her silence too far. Besides, regardless of her dismay toward my apostasy, my mother-in-law, when we were on good terms, once told me that being religious means being kind. I wonder if the irony is lost on her. At least Adam's father is in touch with me. He secretly calls to check on me but has asked me not to tell Adam or my mother-in-law. I have an impulse to call him, with him being my only ally, but I promised I would never call him first in case Adam's mom is sitting beside him.

I turn my cell phone back on. Eight missed calls from Adam and fifteen messages. I check when we last spoke or when he spoke and I said nothing. A mere five minutes ago. I turn my cell phone off once more. I check my email. Another death threat. Oh, and another one. Oh, and another one. After reading these emails, I am glad to be an apostate. I am glad not to be a part of my culture. Is the word culture not etymologically derived from the word cult? I read that somewhere before, and even if it is not true, it has never been truer for me than at this moment. This aggression I am facing from society is cult-like. The treatment of those who leave the fold is cult-like. These are grown men threatening a defenseless woman because she has chosen to live by her own set of beliefs. All I want is the freedom to believe or disbelieve. Is that too much to ask?

There are deranged people out there so intent on making us all the same that they will bully anyone who is different. Well, I do not want to be a part of that club. Even if I offended their fragile egos, there is no excuse for this behavior: madmen writing letters to me, telling me they want me dead, that they are the chosen ones obliged to defend the only true religion, that they are victims of my abuse. Abuse? How did I abuse anyone? They are not victims. They are aggressors. The only victim in this mess was my father. Not my mother. Not my siblings. Not Adam. Just my father. Not even me. At least I can admit to that. I can admit that I, the writer, the honest writer, the activist writer, am a perpetrator. I killed Baba. I am not a victim. I can say it again and again. My name is Dunya, and I am not a victim. How is that for a confession? What about them? Can they admit they are not victims? Can they confess they are perpetrators too?

I open the bedside drawer and reach for the pills. I pour myself a glass of water from the carafe. I swallow two pills. Four. Six. Eight. Ten. It cannot be dangerous to take two more, can it? There is only one way to find out. Two more cannot hurt. What about two more? What about...?

SHE IS awake, I hear someone say. I rub my eyes and try to get up, but my body feels heavy. The room is out of focus. I close my eyes and open them again. I am in a hospital room.

"You're lucky to be alive." This comes from a young-ish doctor with reading glasses perched on his nose.

"Am I alone here?"

"Your husband is here with you. He just popped off to grab something to eat. You're lucky to have a man like him. He saved your life. You were barely breathing when he found you. He hasn't left your side since."

Lucky? Me? He has no idea how unlucky I am. If he only knew...

"Since when? How long have I been here?"

The doctor looks at a piece of paper, tapping on the clipboard. "Two days," he says, squinting, though I cannot imagine why. I mean he is still wearing his glasses. Maybe he needs an eye test to confirm what is obvious to me: the need for a new pair of glasses with thicker lenses.

Adam walks into the room. He greets the doctor and smiles at me. He asks me to move a little. I find it hard to move but I oblige, pushing my hands against the bed to slowly raise my torso and scoot over close to the edge of the bed. He lies down beside me, holding my hand. Has he forgotten our issues? Is he not surprised I am awake? I have been knocked out for two days. No welcome back? Nothing? And why is he now telling me how much he loves me? Did it take me being on the brink of death for him to know my worth? Am I suicidal? This last question grabs my attention, a new problem for my brain to cope with, a Rubik's cube to solve. My husband must sense my anguish: he squeezes my hand and tells me everything is going to be just fine.

I DRIFT in and out of sleep. Between these dozing sessions, my husband fills me in. He came home that afternoon right after we spoke on the phone, or, to be more precise, when he spoke and I said not a word. After trying to get through to me and finding my cell phone switched off, he rushed to our marital home only to find me in bed, barely breathing, mouth foaming, tongue hanging out, arm dangling, a bottle of pills, half empty, on the floor. After trying and failing to wake me up, he called an ambulance, and I was rushed to the hospital. I had overdosed.

"Is this a shyki—?" My speech is slurred. I cannot even say *psychiatric*. "Am I in a shykiyatric ward?"

"No, but I think you should consider going to one. You've been through a lot. Look, I know you must be thinking about our last discussion, but I'm not leaving you. No way. No frickin' way. Forget about everything I said before. You're my wife and that means for better or for worse. I am not going to let you fall apart like this knowing I could've helped you."

Oh, I wish I could believe him. My wishy-washy Adam. I rest my head on his chest as he strokes my shoulder blade. Oh, my Adam has come around, my beloved

Adam. Or has he? Arranged or unarranged, wishy-washy or stable, I adore him. The greatest love of my life. Though that cannot be accurate since I have nobody to compare him to. I do not know what it is like to be with another man, but this feels like the greatest, *he* feels like the greatest. It is an amazing feeling to have someone stick around after threatening to leave. The idea of losing Adam again makes me shudder. He rubs my forearm. What a smile he has. I want to tell him I am sorry for what I have put him through. I want to write him a love letter. I want to beg him never to mention leaving again. But he is massaging my head now, and I do not want to distract him. My arm is hurting from where the drip is inserted, and every time he moves closer I wince from the pain, but I do not tell him because I want to feel his body next to mine.

I know I cannot go on like this. But Adam has given me a newfound sense of faith. Oh, what is this now? I can hear the chorus in the background tugging at my faith, pulling it away from me, telling me only the pills can help, that my husband will leave me, that he is only here because he feels responsible, and soon I will be alone. All alone. I try to silence my thoughts. Yes, I am strong, but I know I need help.

"Oh my God, D! What are you doing?" Adam's voice is trembling.

I look at him, to where his eyes are fixated. I am scratching my forearms and they are bleeding. I scratch some more. I stare at my hand. The finger pads have blood on them from the scratches. I wipe the blood on my cheek and begin laughing. I am aware of this. I cannot be crazy if

I am aware I am acting crazy, right? I mean, I can stop this, but I do not. Or maybe I cannot. There is a thin, dangerous line between do not and cannot. Is my sanity based upon semantics?

"Baby, you're scaring me," he says, getting out of bed, looking around. But is Adam saying he is afraid or is the chorus singing on his behalf? He calls for a nurse. His voice sounds urgent. "Nurse! Nurse!" Why is he so afraid? Now he is scaring me. Am I losing control? Does he see something I do not? I need a mirror. But reflections lie sometimes, do they not? Stop looking at me like that, I try to say, but he is gone. I want to call for a nurse, but again nothing comes out of my mouth.

I feel a tsunami raging forth inside me. Sirens blaring, wailing, sounding. I yank the drip out of my arm and am running, running down a corridor. "Get me out of here," I hear myself yelling. Is it me or the chorus? It is me. Oh no. It is not. Can anyone hear me shouting? Am I shouting?

I stop to catch my breath. Nurses are scrambling, a doctor grabs me by the shoulders, Adam is telling me to calm down, while someone injects a syringe into my arm. Is it the doctor or the nurse? Or is it Adam? Or am I injecting the syringe into myself? The faces, the faces look at me. I know something is wrong, but I wish I could tell them to stop looking at me that way. I hear myself wail. Other patients come out from other wards to peer at me in the hallway, pretending to be concerned—but I am sure they are drawn to the drama. Would you not be? Another syringe. Or is it just a double dose? This one I like. Oh, yes. Give me more of this. Yes, it is okay. Everything is okay. Sweet numbness! It is about to become a chorus, this numbness, but it does not want to sing nor chant nor speak. It is too blissful to ruin the moment with language. Adam is holding my hand. I know I am in a stupor, but I am also in love with the feeling, in love with Adam, in love with the nurses, all four of them now, and the two doctors. I love them all. And I love the way they are coaxing me back to the ward, to the bed, to the pillow I am now resting on, and to the sleep that awaits me.

MONTHS HAVE passed, approaching a year. And I still do not remember much of what happened that day in the hospital after my blackout. But I owe it to you to fill you in on what I remember after the incident.

After spending a few nights in the hospital ward under close, bordering on suffocating, observation—code for suicide watch—I was interrogated by a persistent doctor. I was asked if there was any history of mental illness in the family. I remember telling the doctor who I was, the apostate who got arrested, and he said he knew who I was, everyone did, but he asked me again: "Is there any history of anxiety or depression in your family?" I said no and told him that my father had died. He said he knew. He also knew that my mother and siblings were not talking to me. And he knew that my husband had threatened to separate from me. But he still wanted further explanation. All that, doctor? I would not be human if I did not collapse after all that. He asked again whether there was a history of mental illness in the family disregarding all the reasons I provided that warranted my breakdown with a wave of his bony, café au lait hand.

"No, as far as I know, there is no history of mental illness in my family."

"Have you ever had psychiatric treatment?" he asked.

"No."

He suggested I meet with a therapist regularly until I got my feet back on the ground. I told him I would rather spend time at a psychiatric retreat. He smiled and said that was a great idea, and even my beloved Adam agreed. After leaving the hospital, I looked for options abroad: the landscapes and views of a few of them were splendid. One building looked like a resort, perched on a hill overlooking the Pacific Ocean. But California was too far away for me right now. Adam said he would accompany me. But the thought of flying for more than sixteen hours to reach any destination, no matter how picturesque, dissuaded me. Not in my fragile state. I love flying, I love traveling, I love California, I have been there several times, but I just could not see myself so far away from home right now. Germany was closer, or should I go to England? The truth was that I had no strength to travel anywhere. I was exhausted, physically and mentally.

I began looking for local options. There was a new state-of-the-art psychiatric retreat in town, a twenty-minute drive from my marital home. My doctor said he would do the necessary paperwork for me. I was admitted a week later.

They gave me my own room, courtesy of Adam's uncle who knew someone who knew someone. My mornings and nights were a succession of pills I did not want to take and pills I looked forward to taking. I had constipation one day, diarrhea the next. And, on most days, I suffered from nausea, stomachaches, or headaches. I was given pills to counteract the side effects of the medication. But I could not find a pill to cure my heartache. Still, in spite of all my loneliness, I did not want to see anyone. I wanted to be alone. Alone with the nurses, doctors, and the pills I looked forward to taking. The view was unspectacular. Beyond the barred window, a desert and a yellow brick compound in the distance, the only signs of life. Sometimes I heard a car engine. Otherwise, there was no sound: no birds chirping, nothing. I once heard a goat bleating; however, it could have been my imagination. I had a few hallucinations one night in that ward. There was a terrifying one with my father sporting red horns. And another of my mother dressed in a wedding gown, dripping with blood, torn to shreds. When I told the nurse, she said it was not the pills, that I had a high fever. For a brief moment, I panicked. Was I dying? Did I have an incurable virus? I usually know when I have a fever. Was the nurse lying to me about having a fever? Were they trying to kill me in here? Were they making me sick? Were they going to hurt me? Was the nurse working for agents who were out to get me? Or maybe it was the doctor who interrogated me at the hospital. He seemed eager to get me a room here. But wait... I chose this place. He was fine with me going to any retreat, even abroad. No, I do not think he wants me dead. He could have killed me at the hospital. It would have been much less of an ordeal for him.

That night, I shivered in bed, tossed and turned. My bones ached. I felt the fever, and I made a promise to myself never again to mistrust the nurse here or the doctor at the hospital who was not plotting my murder from a distance. I made a promise to myself never again to mistrust any doctor or any nurse. They were medical staff with integrity rooting for my recovery. Do nurses take the Hippocratic oath too? I wonder. No more paranoia. No more. Why did I feel paranoia in the first place when I was taking medication for everything under the sun? Was the paranoia another side effect? Or was I so sick that even pills could not appease my insanity? Insanity? Oh no. Was I insane? I could not be insane if I knew I was. Right?

The fever took over my body and my cells held the fort and fiercely fought the invader with the help of paracetamol and other pills the names of which I cannot recall. My body, via profuse sweating and shivering, and my mind—through a couple more hallucinations involving my brother and sister attempting to smother me with a pillow—competed for my attention. My body won. I was too preoccupied with fighting my fever to even considering fighting my thoughts.

And I remember a succession of visits to a therapist. Who? Dr. Zahra, a psychiatrist in her forties. She wore open-toed high heels and was decked in designer clothing. I must admit she was impressive (and not just aesthetically). She helped me face my demons. I am far from being cured, but she opened something inside of me, a portal to recovery so to speak. Yes, the pills she prescribed helped: there was one for psychosis and paranoia, one for anxiety, another one for depression. Pink, blue, yellow. And a white pill for emergencies. I liked the white one, but as time elapsed—five long, dark-night-of-the-soul months—I stopped taking the white one. And a few months later, my stunning therapist weaned me off all the pills. Adam bought the pills from the pharmacy, as stipulated by Dr. Zahra, and kept them hidden away. When I complained to Dr. Zahra, she said she was the one who asked Adam to keep the pills away from me, it was just bureaucracy. I asked her if she trusted that I would not overdose again, and she said she had complete faith I would not. And at that moment, that is all that mattered. Her faith. Her professional faith, to boot.

Still, even after I had been taken off the pills, Dr. Zahra insisted the therapy go on. The grief had subsided, but my anger toward my mother, husband, and siblings emerged.

Oh, and one important thing I forgot to mention that will help justify why I am so angry. When I came out of the psychiatric ward, and just a day or two before I started seeing Dr. Zahra, Adam told Mama about my nervous breakdown. I was upset at him, but slightly more upset at my mother for telling him that if he ever mentioned me again, she would stop speaking to him. Oh, but I was most upset at Adam for telling me that my mother said I am dead to her. How brutal to hear those words! Why did he have to tell me that? How callous of him! Dr. Zahra said it was his way of letting me know that the bridges had been burned between my mother and me. I had to accept it as a reality.

"So, she'll never talk to me again?" I asked her.

"Well," Dr. Zahra responded, "time will tell. For now, let's focus on your wellbeing. Let's get you strong enough to be okay whether or not your mother is in your life. Okay?"

"Yes, Dr. Zahra. Okay." I wanted to tell her anything she said would be okay by me.

I will do my best to identify any other flashbacks or significant memories that may arise, if and when applicable, but maybe I will not need to. Who knows? All in all, I am sure the timeframe will be clear, even with my scattered mind. And if it is not, forgive me. I am not saying the past and the present are a blur—that is not what I am saying at all. But if time elapses, and there is a need to fill in the temporal blanks, I will do my best to, even at the expense of disrupting a linear timeframe. I apologize in advance.

So here I am, having survived detainment, the death of my father, the disappearance of my siblings, the abandonment by my mother, marital strife, feelings of guilt about writing, feelings of dismay for not writing, a brief stint in the hospital and at a psychiatric ward, therapy, colored pills, and the white magic pill, and no pills. My husband and I are back on track, albeit a track on shaky terrain, in the sense that we are on good terms, but he worries too much about me, which is a good thing now that I think about it, given how much I cherish his attention. But it is also a bad thing because I am not considering another overdose though he suspects otherwise. He once asked if I had planned the overdose, and I, the honest wife, told him that I surprised even myself, having had no idea I would take all those pills until the moment I did. So, I do not blame him for being worried. What if I have another moment of unplanned weakness? But I will not. No, I will not. I pray he believes me. I will prove it to him. But I must prove it to myself first. How?

Oh, this morning—see? a flashback! a recent flashback—Dr. Zahra suggested I write a letter to my mother. She told me I should not send it, but it is important to address my feelings on paper, as it will be cathartic. She also said I should write a letter to my father. "Writing makes you feel good and it's important to give your feelings an outlet." That is what she said to me. Now, as I ponder her suggestion to write to my mother and father, tears flow down my cheeks. Sentimental tears, nostalgic tears. These tears are not for my mother or my father. They are for my writing. Of course, I miss my parents, but I also miss writing. And I especially miss writing for the public: the feedback, the feeling of having an article approved for publication. Whenever I go out, random people I bump into ask me whether I am going to write again.

It is strange being this famous. People are always taking selfies with me and tagging me on social media. At restaurants with Adam, we get glared at sometimes. But mostly, I have fans. So many fans. From all over the world. And famous journalists, activists, and writers commemorate me on their websites and blogs. There are countless articles about me online, but I only check once a week, or once a fortnight, because I hate reading negative comments about me from trolls and haters. I can have a hundred positive comments, but one negative comment sticks to my mind like a fly in a web. But I cannot hate the haters, nor judge them. The haters speak the same language as the voices in my head that berate me, the voices I try to drown out with therapy, the voices I tried to drown out with pills. To be fair, the voices are more silent lately, but once in a while, a paranoid thought emerges uninvited, and to regain balance I take a walk. Dr. Zahra told me that exercise is a form of therapy. Exercise and fresh air. And boy is she right! Walking has saved my life.

Dear Mama,

I still do not understand why we are not in touch. Something is warped, Mama. The strongest bond in the world is between a mother and her daughter. I lived in you for nine months. We were joined by an umbilical cord, Ma. That kind of bond never breaks, even when the cord is cut. You know that. I know that. It is nature. And by not talking to me, you are tampering with your maternal instinct. Mama, you used to tell me about mothers whose grown children were first-degree murderers but who never gave up on their kids, visiting them in prison, fighting for their release. When I asked how it was possible for anyone to love a murderer, you told me I would not understand until I was a mother.

Mom, if you think that I murdered Dad, if you truly believe that, well according to your logic, you should still love me. I am that grown child who went to prison, I am that grown child who killed her father. And mine is not even first-degree murder, yet you refuse to talk to me.

I have so much pain inside of me. I am not trying to play the victim, but I miss you so much, sometimes I feel I could die of grief for you. Tell me: How do you do it? How can you stay away from me? I can barely sleep or eat. My life is being lived on autopilot. Every day, hope and despair battle for ownership inside of me. And both my hope and despair revolve around you. I am such a mess, such a mess.

I blame myself for the death of Baba, and I know I will for the rest of my life, therapy or no therapy, but you are supposed to comfort me. You are supposed to tell me that it is not my fault Baba died, even when we both know it is. That is what mothers do. They lie to make their children feel better. Right?

But if you cannot do that for me, for your child, then I will comfort you.

Maybe you need to hear it from me over and over again: yes, I killed Dad. Yes, I killed Dad. Yes, I killed Dad. Does that make you feel better? Because it makes me feel better knowing it might make you feel better. Tell me what you feel. Shout at me. Yell at me. Hit me. Slap me. But do not ignore me, Mama. Your silence is killing me. Maybe that is what you want, to torture me, to make me pay for taking away Baba. But I did not mean it. That we both know. If the entire world were a jury, they would not indict me for the murder of Baba, even when I contradict myself and say I killed him. Yes, he is dead because of me, but I take back that I killed him. No I did not kill him. Please have mercy on me, Mama.

Adam has been an angel, telling me that it is not my fault, but both you and I know it is. And so what can I say? I am sorry. I will repeat this again and again. I hope that by repeating it I am not annoying you. If I am, then please forgive me for that too. Forgive me for being born. Forgive me for growing up into a rebellious writer. But I ask not for your forgiveness regarding the murder of Baba. This was not murder even though he is dead because of me. This was a consequence of my foolish action.

Mama, I am not proud of what I have written in the papers. But I stand by my principles, and though I do not regret being an apostate, I regret having published that article, not only because of what I wrote, but because of how it affected you all. I do not care what people think, I never have, Mama. You know that, you raised me. I only cared in public because you taught me to care. You raised us to care. But you know that I really did not care. That is why writing came so easy to me.

Remember when the article was published, and you were upset I had not told you about it prior to publishing it? I asked whether you would have stopped me if you had known about it beforehand, and you said no. Do you remember telling me how excited Baba was? He was proud of me, you said. And the lawyer told me how much you supported me when I was detained, and Adam told me things only changed after Baba's demise. It feels so surreal knowing he is dead. But believe it or not, with all my grieving for Dad, it is worse knowing that you are alive and I cannot see you. It kills me that you tell Adam I am dead to you. Mama, why are you doing this? Why are you treating me like a criminal? Why?

I will reiterate this over and over again: I need you. I love you. I adore you. I grieve for you. I rage. I lament. I regret. I am in pieces over this. Please find it in your heart not just to forgive me, but to remember that life is unpredictable and sometimes things happen that shock us, hurt us, but we are family, flesh and blood, mother and daughter.

I will never, ever get over not speaking to you, Mama. Know that: never! A part of you is and will remain with me every step of the way, in my body, in my limbs, in my soul, in my heart, and in my mind. You are my mother and you dwell in a lofty realm within me.

Mama, remember how I used to lie down beside you during your afternoon naps and brush your hair? And how I would sit on a stool in the kitchen while you cooked, your very own personal taster? You are a great chef, but I will say this: if you had cooked cardboard and sprinkled it with sawdust and mice whiskers, it would have tasted delicious to me.

Remember what you said when I got married: You are leaving this house, but your home is always here and you pointed at your heart. You and Dad spoke of an invisible thread that joins us as a family. It is unbreakable, you both insisted. You said that marriages collapse but nothing can destroy the foundation of parents and their offspring.

I know you are grieving, and I know how grief works. I have surprised myself with my own madness lately, creeping up on me when I least expect it. I, like you, have wailed, have screamed, have been overcome with anger and despair so profound I do not know how much more I can take. But you are the glue that can piece together the broken vase that is me now. Mama, you are the seed I need right now in order to flourish and grow. You are water and fertilizer. You are even the sun that nourishes me. You are everything to me. My everything.

I will stop now, but I want you to know that I will never cut the thread that binds us together. I pray that you soon remember I am a daughter who adored, and adores, and will always adore her father. And I pray that you soon remember I am a daughter who adored, adores, and will always adore her mother. You know that. Mom, I beg you to remember who I am to both Baba and you. I am the fetus that was once inside you. I am the infant, the toddler, the child, the adult, all rolled into one, asking you to forgive me, to love me once again, to welcome me back into your arms and your life.

P.S. I went back and read the letter again and excuse me for rambling throughout. I am not going to edit this letter no matter how nonsensical it may read. And besides, I will probably throw this away soon. I might show it to my therapist. Who knows? Anyway, apart from the I killed Baba, no I did not, I think it is a pretty good letter because each word, each line, so obviously screams out what I am yearning to say: I LOVE YOU!

With all the love and adoration and respect I can muster and more,

Dunya

I CALL Alice. She is whispering, telling me she can't talk right now, Mama might overhear her. I have a letter for Mama, I say. She tells me she will call me later and hangs up the phone. I will wait right beside my cell phone for her to call back. I will wait until the phone becomes my second skin. I cannot believe I have the courage to give Mama the letter. Dr. Zahra may be disappointed with me, but after a night of tossing and turning, unable to decide whether I should throw the letter away or give it to Alice to give to Mom, I made up my mind. I am scratching my cuticles again. And now picking at them. Oh darn, the nail bed of my index finger is bleeding. I walk to the medicine cabinet and dab some Fucidin cream on it and cover it up with a Band-Aid. My mom had advised me when I was growing up that I should let it breathe, but I like the way the cream soothes my skin and the Band-Aid helps the germaphobe in me to relax.

Oh, here is a message from Alice: "Sorry I did not call back. I still cannot talk now. Drop off the letter at six p.m." I look at the time. It is sixteen minutes past noon. Okay, 6:00 p.m. In the meantime, I can write a letter to my Baba.

Dear Dad,

Oh, where do I begin? I feel so much guilt, Dad. All I can think of now is the way you raised me. You were always good to me. You never laid a finger on me. You never shouted at me. And though I heard you and Mama arguing once behind closed doors, I respect the fact that you never argued in front of me or in front of Yasser and Alia. And it is not like you were shouting, I just happened to pass by your room to ask you something and overheard you. Just once. Imagine that. That is probably a record for other families. And just to let you know, I was not eavesdropping. Or was I? Oh, why am I writing about this? There is so much more I want to say to you, about how much I miss and love you, but Dr. Zahra, my therapist, has told me to write without censoring my thoughts. I could do with a bit of stream of consciousness. Here is what would come out:

Dark. Tree. Finger branches, gilded leaves. A luminescent puddle. Random thoughts. People chattering, here is a Siamese cat, there is a pug, the neighbors are afraid, the sun is coming out, but now it is shy, hiding behind clouds. Potluck. Peanut shells, elephant tusks. Paper tigers, butterflies. Skipping on the pavement. Yes. No. What is an aphorism? Why is it blue when it is black? Where is the platypus hiding? Blue shoes, a rainbow. Ha ha. Here is the way to another way. Distributor. Full moon. Jade. Eyes of the gazelle. Ruby. Lion. Lit. Prosperity. Virgin Mary. Skilled. Love. Joyful. Meadow of ash trees. Prince. Bright One. Bee. A. An. The. In a while. Quotation marks cradling miniature dolls. Hello. Adieu. James Joyce. Proud. Virginia Woolf. Elated. Life is grand. Beaten stick. Stick beating. Bruises. Eyes closed, open. Gunshots and reveries. Here I am loving you, Dad. Here I am. In all these thoughts you are here. A window. A door. A creek. A brook. Waterfalls. Elation.

WHEN THE HABOOB SINGS

Okay, I am certain an analyst would have a field day with what I just wrote. Dad, this is the stupidest letter ever. I am so ashamed that I, the writer, cannot even write a proper letter. A proper letter to you would have gone like this:

Dear Baba,

I am so sorry. I know if you had survived your heart attack, you would not have blamed me for it, but you are not here to defend me and you are dead; so, for the rest of my life, this feeling of guilt will plague me. It's weird. We all know guilt is a stage of grief. But, my guilt is eternal. It will never go away, Daddy. At the risk of sounding melancholic, might I add how gloomy life is without you? Still, I am grateful. Because I feel your love, dead or alive. And I want to thank you for supporting my article. It was great to know you were proud of me when much of the world was against me. I want to thank you for trying to visit me while I was in jail. I think I would have jumped for joy had I seen you entering my cell. The greatest punishment, more than the loneliness

I felt in jail, was being deprived of seeing you. They got me there. They hit me right where it hurt. And if someone out there wanted me to feel sorry for writing the article, all I have to do is remember you and be filled with regret. Oh, Baba! To know that you were a few feet away from me kills me. To know you were so close but so far will continue to torment me until I myself die and join you wherever you are. Even if where you are is nowhere.

Oh, how I miss you. Oh, how I need you. Oh, how I love you. Please forgive me. You know what? I know you do. You were always such a kind soul. Stressed, but kind. Generous. Always at ease around everyone. Diplomatic. Eager to please.

Can I ask you for a big favor Baba? Can you please visit Mama in her dreams and tell her to forgive me? Can you also tell Yasser and Alia in their dreams to get in touch with me?

And please continue to visit me in my dreams, Dad. The other night I dreamed you were dressed in white and sitting in the passenger seat of a golf cart. I was driving the cart on a green lawn.

WHEN THE HABOOB SINGS

To our left was a large white hotel. It was massive. And I remember being aware it was a dream and asking you what the afterlife was like and you said it was amazing. Oh, Dad, I am so glad you are happy. And I do not know whether the afterlife or reincarnation exists, but I hope it does because I want to kiss your hands, your soft hands, your padded hands, and I want to massage your chubby feet. And I hope you never come back to this Earth if reincarnation exists. I want you to be in a place where there is no judgment, no pain, no stress, and no such thing as death. I want you to be in a place where forgiveness does not exist because nobody is ever upset to begin with. Oh, come back to me, my beloved Father.

I love you so much.

Love,
Dunya

Yes, Baba, that is the proper letter I should have written in the first place. But here I am, still writing the letter that encompasses the letter I should have written to you, so I suppose I am not done. I will never be done writing if I had my way. I could write this letter to you for the rest of my life ad infinitum ad nauseam. I could write until my fingers bled. I could write letters and letters to you and buy stamps and post them to you wherever you are. Where are you, Baba? Or should I be asking: Are you?

Oh, Baba, are you? How do I know you still exist? Will I ever know? Remember what Mama used to say: Who died and came back to tell us about the afterlife?

Oh, I am getting distracted from what I want to say, but I will end it in the same way I ended the proper letter within this letter: I love you so much.

Love,
Dunya

IT IS NOW 6:00 p.m. I am parked outside Mama's home, my parents' home. The home I was raised in still stands, a stately mansion, haunted by the ghost of my father. This is cheating since I can see the house before me, but here is a description: yellow bricks, a two-story house with a manicured lawn, hedges in the shapes of animals—a rabbit, a giraffe, and a Sphinx cat. Two lion statues at the front entrance, a large door made of oak, and a brass knocker, gigantic, made for the hands, or the hand, of a giant. The house can be intimidating with its high ceilings, stained glass windows, a spiral staircase (see, I know this well even though I am still not inside, not bad at all), marble floors, and chandeliers in every room, including the bedrooms. The reception room itself looks like it was transported from Victorian England. Mom loves all things English, all things antique. My father's philosophy was: *if you have the money, why not spend it?* And Baba certainly had the money, and Mama had and still has exquisite taste. Yes, we were fed with the proverbial silver spoon and to be quite honest the spoons were platinum. My parents cared more about our education than buying us fancy clothes and material objects, but they still bought us fancy clothes and material objects. They were what you would call good parents. They never hit us. We were never emotionally abused in any way. Alice only helped to raise us, because Mom was always around, what one would call a hands-on parent, helping us with homework, driving us around though we had chauffeurs, talking to us, eating meals with us. Baba, though generous and attentive, was mostly at work. What I do remember is Baba reading to us when he had free time on his hands. He loved reading to us. And whenever he traveled he came back with books as gifts for us. He bought us everything from Naguib Mahfouz to Rabindranath Tagore, Toni Morrison to Albert Camus, Chinua Achebe to Emily Dickinson, Goethe to Sylvia Plath, Thomas Hardy to Italo Calvino, Alice Walker to Haruki Murakami. It was his way of extending a part of him when he was not around.

All in all, we were lucky growing up. Mama and Baba's only paranoia was regarding what they often referred to as *the reputation of a girl*, which is why my sister and I were not allowed to go out unaccompanied by an adult chaperone. My brother Yasser had a lot of freedom though being born with genitalia differing from ours. My parents never berated him for going out. Still, when Mom caught him wearing makeup once after coming home from a party, I overheard her tell him: "I don't care what you are, Yasser, you're my son. But don't ever go out like this in public again. Whatever you want to do, please do it in our house or while you are on holiday, not in our country." And Yasser obeyed. He only wore makeup around the house. And when we traveled. But he stopped wearing makeup altogether on a family trip out yonder to the Western Hemisphere when we were sitting outdoors at a restaurant and a passerby called him a faggot. We had never heard that word before. But what shocked us all was that we thought things were different in the West. Apparently not.

I call Alice to come outside. She has tears in her eyes. "I miss you," she says. "Me too," I respond. She takes the letter. I grab her bony wrist and kiss the palm of her hand before she goes back into the house.

"Update me."

"I will, beautiful," she says. And just as I am about to drive away, she tells me she loves me.

DAMMIT, WHO'S calling now? I look at the time. It is 2:00 a.m. Yasser? No way! I jump out of bed, Adam turns to me: "Who is it?"

"It's Yasser. Oh my God!" I walk toward the living room. "Hello?"

"Hi, Dunya." Does he sound cold or am I imagining it?

"Oh, my love, I miss you so much. How long has it been? Where are you, my love?"

"Your *love*? Are you out of your mind? Stop calling me. Stop harassing me. Leave me alone! Leave Mom alone! Get it through your thick head. She will never talk to you again. To her, you murdered Baba."

"How can you say that, Yasser? It's not my fault—"

"I said *to her*, not to me. Listen before you pounce on me. Look, I know she's irrational in blaming you, but you have to respect her need to be away from you."

"If you know she's behaving irrationally, why do you sound so angry?"

"Because you're selfish. That's the thing with writers. You're all egotists, thinking only of yourselves, not how your writing can affect others. You wanted fame, huh? You wanted people to remember you, and you wanted to leave this legacy behind? Well, guess what, you're not famous, you're infamous, notorious. Let those human rights organizations boost your ego. You are cruel to your own family, so stop pretending you're doing good in this world. You've ruined us, all of us. Stop harassing us and get on with your life. And if you call me back, I'll sue you for emotional distress. Alia wants nothing to do with you either, so stop calling her. And if you write another letter to Mama again, I'll personally deal with you."

"I miss you guys so much. I love you," I say while bawling.

"Stop going into victim mode, Dunya. You're not a victim. Okay? Don't try to make me feel bad. My conscience is clear. Is yours?" The line is breaking, I can hear a few words: *stop—enough—selfish—leave.*

"Yasser, I can't hear you properly. The line is cutting."

"Well—it's—and—heaven's sake—her alone—goodbye."

"What? I can't hear you. Oh, don't say goodbye! Please, Yasser! I'm so sorry. You're my brother. Yasser, I need you. Please!"

Adam makes his way toward me. He tells me to hang up the phone. I cannot. I hear Yasser continue: "Are you happy? Is this what you wanted to hear me say? Mom tried to spare you more pain, but you're a masochist, Dunya. You love pain, such a drama queen. You're toxic. Now leave us the heck alone and get on with your life." And at that, he hangs up on me.

I CALLED Dr. Zahra earlier today to schedule an emergency appointment. She set up an appointment for two hours later. I am now sitting in her office. If I could hole up in this room for the rest of my life, I would. I would not leave. Ever. Dr. Zahra is the only person I feel who puts me back together again, albeit transiently. She is the only person, apart from my best friend Layla, who has stayed faithful to me throughout my highs and lows. I know it is her job, but I still appreciate her. In her presence, I do not crack—I reassemble myself, or she reassembles me. And the minute I walk out of the door, I cannot wait to be in her presence again. Therapy is a miracle. Dr. Zahra is a miracle. And around her, I am a miracle.

I am fidgeting with my cuticles again. Dr. Zahra never tells me to stop when I do, but she has a way of looking at my fingers first, after which she looks at me, and just like that, I leave my cuticles alone. I tell her about the letter and how I did not want to send it initially but ended up giving it to Alice to deliver to my mom anyway. And then I tell her about Yasser's call. Dr. Zahra does not say a word, but I am sure she must be disappointed. I search for clues that she is upset, but she is nodding, listening to me. I know I should have listened to you, I tell her.

"Let's deal with this moment and not what you should have done or should not have done," she says. How articulate. How intelligent. I look at her. She is beautiful. I look around the room. It is a bright and airy office on the twenty-first story with floor-to-ceiling windows overlooking the sea. It must be great to be her. I am not envious, just wistful. I wish it felt great to be me. Why was I born me? Why can I not have a dream job like Dr. Zahra, helping people, giving them wings, guiding them back to sanity? Why can I not be the normal one like her, fixing people like me who are not so normal? Why did I have to court controversy? Why did I have to be a writer? Okay, yes. I love writing. Yes, I do. But why did love bring me so much hate?

On the way back home, I call Layla. We have known each other since we were four. She is my only friend. I have always been an introvert, but the truth is that, even when I tried to be an extrovert, even when I tried to fit in with the popular girls at school, I was always ostracized.

And so I stuck with Layla. She held my hand when the world turned against me. She was not allowed to visit me in prison, but she still made her way to the police station two times, sometimes three times a week, trying to see me. You might be surprised that I hardly mentioned her. Well, maybe I *am* a drama queen like Yasser said. Maybe I spend too much time focusing on all the bad things that have happened since my imprisonment. Well, Layla's a good thing. She called my mother more than once and tried to make peace between us. Layla did not visit me at the psychiatric hospital, because she was not informed about it until after I was released. And so here I am at Layla's place. And though she is a good thing, I still feel broken. She does not have Dr. Zahra's soothing effect on me. But she is the closest thing I know to unconditional love, and what is better than that?

"What's on your mind?" she asks. Layla is sitting across from me in her bedroom suite, her on a white wicker chair, and me on a comfortable sofa, beige.

"I want to write again," I tell her.

"So write." She uncrosses her legs. Her legs are long, lithe. She is wearing white ballet flats, a gray pleated skirt, and a pink tank top. This description thing. Quite getting the hang of it, no?

"But you know my writing. I can't tame it."

"Well, let me ask you this: what do you have to lose?" she asks.

I do not have an answer for that. She is right. I lost my father, my mother, my brother, my sister. And if Adam ever decides to leave me again, I will lose him too. But I ask myself her question with a twist of lime: What do I *not* have to lose? My writing. And Layla. And Dr. Zahra.

I tell her my brother thinks I am an egotist. And she responds: "Aren't we all?"

Again, she is right.

"Well?" Layla prods.

"Well, what?"

"Well, are you ready to stop being so hard on yourself? You are a good soul, D. You always have been. You're conscientious, kind. And what I adore about you the most is your loyalty. Why can't you see what a great person you are?"

Okay, so what is good about me? Let us see. I have not cheated on my husband, I have never killed anyone (no I did not kill my father, okay maybe I did, oh, I do not know whether I did or did not; but anyway, if I did, then it was unintentional and if I did not then I have never killed anyone), I do not steal, and I try not to lie. I was not rebellious growing up, was an obedient student and daughter, read voraciously. I got good grades, was neither suspended nor given detention. Back to the present: I am quiet, a good person overall (whatever that means), and devoted to my inner circle. Overall, I am not such a bad person. I can lose my temper, yes. I pout, I keep my distance from people—I try to get close, but I repel people and am simultaneously repelled by them, which works for both sides since nobody wants to get close to me and I do not want to get close to anyone, apart from Layla, Adam, Dr. Zahra, and my immediate family. All those years of behaving well, of being an ideal daughter, were obliterated by one article.

Layla is looking at me. She asks if I am ready to write and embrace my talent for expressing myself. I tell her I will not write about apostasy ever again, that is done, but I will not stop writing. People will always be offended by what I write, I add. So I might as well write something. She nods her head and smiles. I love her.

SIDENOTE: BEFORE being imprisoned, I had heard about an illegal pregnancy ward in my country. It is located in a wing in one of our local hospitals, and it is a ward for women who "broke the law" by getting pregnant out of wedlock. Nobody is allowed to enter the ward apart from nurses and midwives. Security men guard the entrance. But the thing I love about my country is that we are only one phone call away from being granted a favor. An uncle in the ministry, an aunt working at an embassy, cousins in the police force, you name it. Just one call away. Only one degree of separation in my beloved homeland. Two at most. Okay, maybe three degrees in extreme cases.

    I called my uncle who just happened to have a friend who had a friend—yes, an extreme case—who worked in the Ministry of Interior. A few phone calls later, I was granted access to the ward. "Done," my uncle said. Remember, this was before my imprisonment, so my family members still treated me with love and were not afraid of my writing. I told him I wanted to do a feature, and he said it was a great idea but not to make it obvious. I visited the place, without a notebook and pen, without a laptop. I, the writer, the sensitive one, cried while holding one of the ladies who was seven months pregnant. Her name was Ivy. She whispered that the man she slept with lied to her and told her they would get married, but when he found out she was pregnant, he stopped talking to her and answering her calls. She tells me the lady in the ice-blue nightgown two beds down from her—Martha—was raped by her employer. After giving birth, both Ivy and Martha will face a brief "trial" proclaiming their guilt and will be deported immediately with their babies in tow. I asked her why the woman who was raped was being prosecuted and she said her employer's wife begged the lady not to mention that her husband had raped her, and when she refused to get an abortion, she was fired and arrested. Martha never told anyone, except Ivy, about the rape. When the police asked her who she had slept with, she answered it was a man she met on her day off and she had no idea who he was. They called her a prostitute and a cheap woman, handcuffed her and brought her to the ward.

I never published the article about the pregnancy ward as I got sidetracked by other articles, but this is the piece I will send to editors abroad. Yes, it is time to revive my activism. And I am staying away from local papers for now.

I AM going through all the offers that were presented to me since my imprisonment. The top papers and magazines in the world have been vying for a piece from me or about me. As long as I stay away from writing about apostasy or my experience in jail, I am safe. No legal trouble.

I will write for many of them, but now, I send out an email to the most-read paper in the world. Yes, the most-read paper in the entire world. I am not exaggerating. In my part of the world, if you are imprisoned, on a banned list, or lashed, the world will give you attention. Thankfully, I was never lashed, but I ticked the other boxes. I check the date of the email: it was about four months ago. I hope they are still interested in featuring my writing.

Adam walks in. "Whatcha doin'?"

"Nothing," I reply. I am worried he will not approve of me writing again. I can tell him later when the paper agrees to publish my article.

Finally, hours later, I am reading a response. The editors of the most-read newspaper in the world are intrigued by the article about the ward and have agreed to publish it, but I have to agree to a special report featuring yours truly. I mention the NDA, and they tell me there is a way around it. They will write a report about me, using a "source" to reveal the mystery shrouding my imprisonment and consequent release. The source will also reveal why I have not spoken out about my time in jail, and what I am up to now. When I email back asking him who the source is, he responds by informing me the source is none other than me and am I available for a Skype call?

We email back and forth and agree on a time. I choose a time when I know Adam will be at work.

The interviewer is a man in his forties named Alex. Should I describe him? Okay, here goes. He has chestnut-blond hair, big (and I mean big) blue eyes, and thin lips, and he moves a lot while speaking. He moves his phone a lot too, and I am now speaking to a blank white wall for a couple of seconds. Before he puts the phone back to his face, I can see his hand scribbling. He is so busy writing what I am saying that he does not notice we cannot even see each other. Maybe a voice call would have been better. I am distracted by all the movement: Alex, the wall, Alex, the wall, Alex's hand, Alex's notebook, Alex's forehead, Alex's pen, Alex, the wall.

One Skype call is not enough for jittery Alex, the scribbler. He asks for another call. I suggest a voice call, but he insists he prefers video calls. Okay, I find myself saying, though I wish I had been more assertive. I do not like video cameras. I never have. I prefer to communicate via writing and speech.

Two Skype calls later, and Alex and I are good to go. He tells me he will send the article beforehand for approval. I am restless to read it. I can feel my heartbeat accelerate when he tells me it will come out soon. What does soon mean? But I cannot ask, I do not want to appear eager. I am nervous but excited. I cannot remember the last time I felt so alive. Okay, I feel alive in Dr. Zahra's office. But that is different. That is a peaceful kind of alive. I now feel exhilarated, ecstatic. But my exhilaration is swiftly clouded by my fears. What will Mama think? Will she be more upset at me? What about Yasser? Layla? Adam? It does not matter. It is too late. And, besides, it is worth the risk to be published in such a prestigious paper, and I want people to know about the illegal pregnancy ward.

IT HAS been two weeks, two whole weeks, of incessantly, obsessively checking my email, and here it is, here it finally is before me, an article titled *Dunya Khair: Apostate Gone Wild*. Hmm, I am not a fan of the title. I read it to make sure the source does not sound like me. I hope not. Alex stayed true to everything I said, no embellishments, no twisting of the truth. Well, of course it is accurate, what better source than the source herself? Wink, wink. He asks me to approve the article so they can print it in the next day's paper. It will come online right away, he adds in the email. I write him back saying I approve. I do not bother mentioning the title, as I do not want to delay the appearance of the article.

Alex is right about it coming online right away. The special report about me comes out about ten minutes after I email Alex approving the article. It mentions my non-disclosure agreements, my time in prison, and my father's death, and it goes on to mention my estrangement from my mother and siblings, my stint in the hospital, my nervous breakdown and a subsequent brief stay in a psychiatric ward which I included so that nobody would suspect it is me. It mentions my overdose, which I now wish I had not mentioned or approved. Oh, well. And the title is a bit overboard, I mean it is hardly wild to write an article about apostasy or to have been admitted to a psychiatric hospital, but I know about sensationalist headlines. They sell.

I send the article to Layla, and when she calls me back and tells me what an amazing article it is and how glad she is that my story is finally out and adds that she hopes I am not upset that my secrets have been revealed and wonders aloud who could have betrayed me, I am relieved. If my best friend cannot tell I am the source, nobody will. I reveal to Layla I am the source. After expressing her surprise—"No way! Oh my goodness!"—she laughs and adds: "Wow! You crazy girl, you! Well done! I feel better knowing that nobody betrayed you. What a great way around the NDAs, sneaky you."

There is no way anyone would suspect I was the source unless they work in the media industry or are famous. I smile and send an email thanking Alex with an attachment of the illegal pregnancy ward article. He replies right away, writing it is not a good idea to publish the article in their paper because it would seem odd that I would choose to publish a piece with them right after they "exposed" me. I tell him I feel betrayed and ask him why he did not tell me earlier that it would look suspicious. I told him we had a deal, but he swears that he did not think about it until earlier this morning. And I believe him. And he is right. People *will* find it odd. I cannot believe I did not even think of that.

WHEN THE HABOOB SINGS

Alex says they will still publish it if I want—after all, it is good business for their paper—but I will lose credibility. Sweet Alex. I thank him for considering my reputation. He tells me he has a friend who works for another paper, also a prestigious paper, read and respected across the globe, and that his friend would publish my article. I tell him to go ahead and send it to the other paper. Here begins the new phase of my career, and nobody, nothing, can stop me now.

I RECEIVE emails from all over the world, some referring to the special report about me, while others mention the article highlighting the illegal pregnancy ward. Many people did not even know the ward existed. They thank me for highlighting such an important and overlooked issue. But, as usual, I have a few death threats calling me a traitor, telling me an apostate has no right to express opinions, and that I better stop writing altogether or face fatal consequences. One person, who I am sure works in the media, writes that he is on to me. It is obvious you are the source, he writes. I do not reply. Not to any of the emails. There are too many and my eyes hurt. I need a break from the screen, so I turn off the computer. I have reached a point where I do not care what the haters say. Am I numb? Maybe. Is this a sign of depression? Perhaps. But I cannot be depressed because a part of me is buzzing, thrilled, excited at the prospect of being a writer again. And I have done too much therapy to fall back into depression. Right?

No matter what happens in the world, it is a great feeling to know that I can write, even in a region like this. I am not letting them take away my greatest passion. No, sir! No, ma'am! They can say what they want, but I will continue to support causes that matter and continue to address injustices that need to be addressed.

Maybe the trolls are jealous, or maybe they are just bored. Their reasons are not my issue. My issue is to ensure I write and write and write. Maybe one day I will write about the haters, the ones on the outside and the ones inside of me. And as for the people who praise me, I want to sit with them in a field, in a crop circle, all of us holding hands, praying collectively for a better world. I want to thank them one by one. Will they ever know how much their love is appreciated and how much I love them in return? They are my saviors, my sources of hope, my lighthouses. They are the Laylas and Dr. Zahras of the world. They are, in short, my tribe. And they are the reason I will continue to write.

MISHAL—AKA Skinny—is calling. I pick up instantly and hear him mutter a quick hello and without waiting for a reply he tells me in an agitated voice that it is not a good idea that I write about anything, that I still need to lay low. He has read the special report about me and says that is not his concern, or anybody's concern for that matter, since I had nothing to do with it—thank goodness he was fooled. But he adds that my article about the illegal pregnancy ward did not come at a good time.

"When is a good time?" I ask.

I can hear hesitation through his silence.

"Hello?" I say.

"Yes, I'm here," Skinny responds.

"Well, when is a good time?" I repeat. He does not say anything, which I take as a cue for me to say something; nature abhors a vacuum.

I tell him that I signed an NDA regarding apostasy, not writing altogether.

"Yes, but you're drawing unnecessary attention to our country," Skinny says.

"Oh, come on, Mishal. Don't be a spoilsport. This is what I write about. I love my country. I see its potential. I know we can do better. And I want foreigners to be less afraid of us, and the only way to do that is by pointing out scary things. When people see we are concerned with cleaning up our mess we appear friendlier. And that ward is scary. There is so much to change here. I want gays to have rights—"

"Oh don't even think about writing about gays. Have you lost your mind? Do you want to be arrested again?"

"I'm not going to write about gays. Well, not just yet. I'm just saying what I want to write about. I wrote that article because I want foreign women here who are sexually harassed and get pregnant, or who have children out of wedlock, to know that they are not criminals. I see a world that's different. I see possibilities, Mishal. I see a world where everyone is treated equally and women aren't sexually harassed. I see a world where I don't need to write about gays or victims of racism or ethnic cleansing because nobody is discriminated against. And if I can't see that world in the real world, let me see it in my writing. Let me strive in my writing. Give me permission to vent."

"I must say you're being dramatic. And I need you to consider what you write. You don't want to be accused of endangering our country. I am here to make sure you don't end up in jail again. Racism, ethnic cleansing. Be my guest and write about those topics. But, gays? Don't go there, Dunya. Don't."

"Are you saying you are against gays?"

"Of course not. My sister is a lesbian. My uncle is gay. I don't care. But I don't run this country. The people who do will lock you up and keep you there."

"Stop talking about jail. Come on. I am not endangering my country. We both know that. I mean, how weak is our country to feel threatened by a writer? Some people will agree with me and some will not. That's life. But just because some people disagree doesn't mean I have to stop writing. Maybe people need to work on their sensitive egos. Otherwise, freedom of speech will become extinct. There's no real threat apart from the dissolution of our egos which is a good thing."

"You're treading on thin ice, Dunya. Don't say I didn't warn you."

"Mishal, if my articles offend people, maybe they shouldn't read them. Life's too short to waste time reading things that might terrify them."

"They're not scared, Dunya. It's just offensive. You know what people are like here," Skinny says. And he keeps talking but I am no longer here. I am in a realm in the afterlife, some sort of paradise, where we high five each other and do somersaults in a galaxy light-years away. A galaxy light-years away where we watch movies about our lives on Earth and laugh. A galaxy light-years away where we tell each other: "Wow, we actually believed that was real?"

"Dunya?" I hear Skinny say.

"Yes, I'm here."

"Okay, I gotta go now. You take care of yourself. And stay away from your computer. Lay low. Please."

I LOOK at the name flashing on my screen and cannot believe my eyes. I answer the phone.

"Hello?" says the familiar voice. The voice from my past. The voice of someone I love so much it hurts sometimes. The voice of someone only a year younger than me. The voice of a person who used to sneak into my room in the middle of the night, get into my bed and cuddle with me, falling asleep in my arms, drooling on me. This is the voice of someone who looked up to me, who bought me perfume and traded clothes with me, who never irritated me one bit when she acted like or copied me, this is the voice of someone who covered for me when I skipped dinner because I wanted to finish a novel in my room.

"Alia? Oh, Alia!" My heart is racing. Tears are flowing down my cheeks.

"How are you, D?"

What a question, I want to say, but I tell her I am fine. She tells me she was with Yasser in London all this time. She is back in town, but he is still there, shacked up with his boyfriend. Are we picking up where we left off? Is she going to apologize for ignoring me all this time? If she wants to act as though nothing happened, I can too. All that matters is that she has called me.

"Does Mom know he's living with someone?" I ask.

"Yes," Alia responds.

"And?" I ask.

"Mom doesn't care that he's gay. You know that."

"Yes, of course, I know that," I respond. "I meant is she cool that he is living with someone in London of all places? There are a lot of locals from here that visit London."

"They keep a low profile as a couple. Their friends are all English, Italian, Brazilian. So it's cool," Alia informs me. "Anyway let's not talk about his love life. He can discuss that with you when you guys make up. Hopefully soon."

Why do we do whatever we want to do abroad as long as we hide who we are here?

I tell her about my painful conversation with Yasser.

"Yes, I know. He told me. But he regrets it, D. He'll come around. I promise you. Just give him time. Dad's death was too much for us to handle. Yasser and I never blamed you for it, believe me, but taking care of Mom was difficult."

"Alia, you didn't take care of Mom. Let's be frank. You were in London with Yasser. She was alone here. I'm sure if you guys were here, we could have resolved everything much faster."

"Look, we needed to get away from Mom too. She was behaving like a psycho, rambling on and on about you being a killer and an infidel. The infidel part made us crack up because she supported you at first and she's hardly religious. But for Yasser and me, it was your imprisonment that was too much. Dad's death just amplified everything. Grief is a monster. We couldn't see clearly. We needed time. And I hope you'll forgive me for abandoning you when you needed me the most." I can hear her bawling.

I tell her how hurt I was by her disappearance and how much I needed her and Yasser. I tell her that I love her and that I forgive her. I am crying. She is crying. There is no space for grudges here. Only love. So much love. I am overjoyed.

I ask her what is, what has been, on my mind: "What about Mom? When can I see her? I miss her so much it hurts."

"She needs time, Dunya. I'm trying to talk some sense into her, but she's just stubborn. I suppose this is her distorted way of dealing with Dad's death."

"Yeah, I guess so. Oh, how I miss you, Alia. Silly Goose." That is what Mom called us growing up. Silly Goose.

She laughs. I laugh. We decide to meet in the afternoon at Zen Zone Café. That place has so many memories for us. And the best chocolate chip cookies in town.

HERE I am, facing Alia. We order cookies and hot chocolate. It is awkward being in her presence. On the phone, it was easy, but now we just look at each other. Still, there is so much love in her eyes, so much love, and I am sure she can see the love in my eyes as well. In moments like this, everything is—how should I say it?—elevated. Do you know what I mean? It is like opening Christmas presents. (Yes, as a pseudo-Muslim family we celebrated Christmas.) It is like Eid celebrations after a month of fasting. I swear I am not exaggerating, but the sky always seemed bluer and the sun brighter during holidays. And this is how it feels now facing my sister. The feeling of peace is overwhelming. You could tell me there was an earthquake on its way, but I would remain calm and die here at this moment, happy, facing my beloved sister.

She tells me about a British guy named Jeremy whom she met in London.

"Oh, are you in love?"

"Yes," she responds, her face flushed. We have never had such a conversation before, so I do not know how to proceed. A boyfriend? How bizarre. Has she...? I shudder at the thought. She could not do such a thing. No she would certainly not!

And instead of asking what is on my mind, my obsession with Mom comes forth: "Does Mom know?"

"I don't think I'm ready to tell her just yet, what with . . ." She does not need to complete the sentence. I know what she means. What with Mom still upset with me... Does Alia want to marry this Jeremy? Mom has always told us to marry our own kind: our tribe, our sect, our nationality. And I obeyed. I, the liberal, rebellious writer, obeyed. But only because I had never considered any other way. (Thankfully, religion was never a stipulation for a spouse, because Mom and most locals take it for granted that any citizen from here is a Muslim. Go figure!) Now, faced with my sister being with someone who is not local, it is absurd that I had not even thought of marrying outside our tribe and sect. Oh, I am happy with Adam, yes I am, happy with my beloved who ticked all the boxes, but nonetheless it is strange that I was so blinded by tradition. Me! I addressed it in my writing when I wrote that freedom means a woman has the right to marry whomever she wants, but that was on behalf of *other* women.

I am even prouder to be Alia's sister now. But I am also dismayed that if she marries him her children will not be given citizenship. She is fidgeting in her chair. Her lips are stained with chocolate. I hand her a napkin gesturing toward her mouth. We laugh.

"Is it serious?" I ask.

"I think so. We adore each other. It's been ten months. I can't see myself with anyone else. I'll fight for him when we are ready to take the next step. But, enough about me. That article you wrote about the illegal pregnancy ward was brilliant. I sent it to Jeremy. He thinks you're a star, by the way. He was desperate for me to get in touch with you. He's been nagging at me for ages."

"Wow. That's touching. But why was he desperate? Were you that against getting in touch with me? Is that why you got in touch? Because Jeremy told you to?" I ask, unable to fathom how Alia could date a man that long before marriage. What happened to conservative Alia? The chorus begins: "It's all your fault. You corrupted your sister. If you hadn't written the article, you wouldn't have gone to jail, your Baba wouldn't have died, your siblings would not have escaped to get away from your drama, and your sister wouldn't have gone to London and met Jeremy."

"No, D. It's not like that. I already explained to you that I needed time. But, yes, Jeremy banged some sense into me. I'm not a robot. Had I disagreed with him, I would've never gotten in touch. He only reflected back to me what I wanted to do." Her eyes are brimming with tears. She is so lovely. Her hair is lighter than it was before. And something about her is different. Is this love? I think of Adam. I love him, yes, but it was hardly a love story. But Alia is glowing. Still, this boyfriend and girlfriend thing is not good. She has to come to her senses. Mama has already suffered at the hands of one of her children (yes to Mama we will always be children). It is too much, too selfish, for Alia to make her suffer more. I want her to marry Jeremy right away, no need for this dating stuff. But I agree it is not the time to tell Mama she is going to be with a foreigner. Nor is it the time for me to preach to Alia.

I ask her a question I was not intending to: "What's his religion?"

She is glaring at me—okay, maybe not glaring—but it is an intense look. I have always had trouble with eye contact, even from my family members. It scares me. I think human beings should not be allowed to look at each other for more than five seconds. I get flustered when someone stares at me, my face heats up, and I even shake in extreme cases, and it looks like I am hiding something or lying and that makes me more self-conscious. Someone can just ask how I am and if they look at me for too long, I blush. Men who I am not attracted to think I am attracted to them or embarrassed about something. But I am not embarrassed. I am flustered. There is a big difference. And when women look at me for too long and I get nervous, they stare more intently, confused by the freak show they are witnessing. What can I say? I am a freak of nature. A shy, anxious, does-not-like-to-be-looked-at-for-more-than-five-seconds freak. Alia is still looking at me. I am sweating under my arms. My face is getting red.

"He's Christian." She bites her lip.

"And?" I feel as though I am invading her privacy, but she brought him up.

"And what?"

"Well, would you want him to convert if you guys end up getting married?"

"No," she answers, a bit too firmly. But she quickly adds: "I mean, he loves his religion, so that wouldn't be fair. He'd have to fake convert, pretend he's Muslim so our papers will be legal. I don't know if he'd agree to that. But if he does, that's great."

This strikes both the chorus and me as strange. Alia is pretty much what one would call a devout Muslim. She prays and fasts. She does not wear the hijab, but she dresses conservatively. But my sister now has a boyfriend and he is Christian and she does not mind? Still, I am proud of her. I am proud that she is religious, but she respects Jeremy enough to honor his belief system as much as she honors her own.

"Have you been intimate with him?" I blurt out, face reddening.

"Of course not! Are you out of your mind? What has happened to you, D? First, you become an apostate and now you think I would let a man touch me before marriage?" She has tears in her eyes. *First, you become an apostate?* That hurts. She must have felt my pain because she reaches out to squeeze my hand and apologizes. I am so glad to be beside her, I tell her to forget about it. I feel terrible for asking whether she was physical with him.

"I'm the one who should apologize, Alia. Please forgive me." We hold hands across the table. This Jeremy situation is gnawing at me. I have more to say about it. Shall I stop? I cannot. She is my younger sister. I have a responsibility toward her. I ask her what she would do if he refuses to 'fake convert.'

"We once had a conversation about religion, and I know he's the kind of guy who won't leave his faith and I respect that because I won't leave Islam either. If he wants me to convert to Christianity, I'll end the relationship, and if he doesn't want to pretend to be a Muslim, it's over too."

I pick at my cuticles. "And you're going to invest more time in him, falling more in love with this guy, only to risk one of you guys breaking up with the other over a decision you should be making now before things get even deeper?"

"D, thank you for your concern," she says, with a hint of annoyance. "But I'm not ready to get married now. I want to wait, get to know him much better, travel around the world with him, see what he's like. I'm on his turf now. I want to see what he's like on mine. Yasser is going to pretend he's a friend of his and he can stay at our house when I'm ready for him to visit. No rush. Maybe a couple of months from now. Who knows? He's dying to meet you by the way. Don't laugh, but he's a fan of your work."

My *work*? I like the sound of that.

"Oh," Alia adds, "And like I said I'm not mentioning anything to Mom now. And not just because of all the drama with you. But because I discussed this with Yasser already. Why tell her about something that may not even materialize?"

"Yeah, I agree. And I understand. It's your life. I'm sure you know what you're doing. Just one more thing. What about if you have children? What religion would they be?"

"That's a loaded question. I can't answer that now, not until I'm sure Jeremy and I are getting married. All I know is I've never felt this way about anyone."

"He's your first relationship. There's nobody to compare him with."

"Still, I know how I feel, and this is love, even if I have nobody to compare him with. Look, let's end this conversation. I don't want to talk about religion or Jeremy or anything serious now. I want to relish this reunion with you." She smiles. And it is Christmas, Eid, Thanksgiving, Easter, Diwali, Vaisakhi, Wesak, and every religious and non-religious festival on Earth at this moment.

IT HAS been more than three weeks since I saw my sister, but we have been in touch every day. And this morning, when she called, she said oh so casually that Mom wants to see me. I had her repeat it more than once until it registered. I even asked her why, thinking this was some kind of trap, that Mama needed to vent some more or needed to face me to tell me how much she hated me. But Alia assured me that Mom is ready to put the past where it belongs. Mom is ready to make peace with me. The word "ready" hurts. But I do not care. I am too excited to care.

When we hung up, I ran to tell Adam, who was in our bedroom, adjusting his headgear for work. He lifted me in his arms and twirled me around the room. He proceeded to waltz me around the house. We were laughing, but I felt anxious, not knowing what to expect.

But now, here I am, wearing a camel trench coat and black leather leggings with orange ballet flats and a fuchsia satchel. And the chorus is singing: "What's going to happen? What will you say? What will Mama say?"

I am trembling and not in any condition to drive, so I ask Adam to take me to Mama's.

Adam parks outside my parents' home and kisses me goodbye. I walk through the manicured lawn to the front door. I have an urge to knock using the giant brass knocker but I do not. I ring the bell. Alice answers. She hugs me, and I nestle my head in her neck. I do not want her to let me go. She has the same smell I have always smelled on her, a combination of liquid detergent and vanilla. Sometimes when she has been in the kitchen, she smells of onions. But not today, thankfully.

I hear footsteps. It is Alia, smiling. I smile back. But it is not Christmas-Eid. I have butterflies in my stomach, and not the good kind. I rush to the bathroom. It is diarrhea.

I can hear Alia asking if I am okay. I unlock the door and she flinches at the smell. Ugh, she says loudly, pinching her nose shut. I smile at her sheepishly and wash my hands in one of the sinks outside the bathroom stall before following her to the living room. Mama is sitting on a couch staring at the blank screen of the television. She looks frail and much thinner than when I last saw her. I search for a smile. Nothing. Her lips are pursed. I look at Alia, who gestures to me to go closer to Mama. I walk toward her and kiss her forehead and take her hands in mine. I kneel to the floor and cry on her lap, but Mom is not moving. Did Alia force her to make peace with me? At least she is not pushing me away, though. Wait a minute! Here it is! She is stroking my hair. I hear a whimper. I look up and Mama is crying, too. And Alia is crying and so is Alice. It is a symphony of waterworks now. I wish Baba were here. Oh, Mama, why did you wait so long to see me?

WHEN THE HABOOB SINGS

And now Mama wipes her eyes and speaks: "I made you eggplant lasagna. Are you hungry?" Am I hungry for my favorite dish from my favorite person? Yes! Yes! Yes!

I respond, feebly, between sobs. "Yes."

Mama gently lifts my chin with her tear-drenched finger and looks at me. She tells me to get up, I do. She gets up from the chair and takes me by the hand, and we walk with Alia toward the dining table. Alice scurries off to the kitchen and returns with two houseboys, all three of them carrying silver platters on silver trays. It is not just lasagna. There are feta cheese cigars and potato and pea samosas. There is Basmati rice peppered with raisins, slivered roasted almonds, and saffron. There is pumpkin and yogurt curry. There is spaghetti Bolognese. There is white rice to accompany the lamb and ladyfinger stew. There are vine leaves stuffed with rice and veal cutlets with rosemary on a bed of mashed potatoes. There is a side table filled with a basket of fruits and carrot cake. There is a pot of tea beside a creamer, a carafe of water, and a jug of Vimto with ice.

There are biscuits, too. I look at my mom, my mom who loves to cook. And I know this is her way of saying: "I love you and I missed you. All is forgiven." There is no need for any explanation, for rehashing what has happened. There is no need for Mama to say she is sorry or for me to ask her for forgiveness. Here, now, I am home again. And what better kind of Christmas-Eid is that? Even with a stomach doing cartwheels.

RIGHT AFTER lunch, we took a nap, Mama and me in the living room and Alia upstairs. I woke up an hour ago and am waiting for Mama to wake up. Alia tiptoed her way to me about twenty minutes ago and told me she was going out and would be back later tonight. So I am alone with my thoughts but relaxed. I look at Mama. She looks stiff, passed out on the antique mustard-yellow couch with the purple tassels. I slept on an antique turquoise couch. These couches are not meant for sleeping on. They are not even that comfortable to sit on. I suppose they were designed specifically for regal Victorian ladies, so they would sit upright on them to maintain their posture when suitors came knocking.

    Mama is stretching. She lets out a loud yawn. There is something so disarming about a person yawning. She is looking at me, smiling. She asks if I want to play cards. Sure, I say. She calls for Alice and tells her to bring us a deck of cards. Mom cannot do anything without Alice. We have three other housemaids, two houseboys, two chauffeurs, two chefs, but for Mom, only Alice exists. When Mom orders the menu for lunch or dinner, she tells Alice, who tells the chefs. When Mom wants one of the houseboys to clean the guest bathroom downstairs, she tells Alice to tell him. When Mom wants the housemaids to clean the rooms and bathrooms upstairs, guess who the go-between is? Oh, and when Mom wants to send a chauffeur out to run errands for her… You get the gist. I do not think I have ever seen Mom address any of her staff directly. Alice has one day off a week, and she once confessed to me that not a day off has passed without Mama texting her for something or the other, trivial things that can wait until she comes home.

"That must be so annoying," I said to Alice.

"Oh, no," she responded. "I like it. It's adorable, endearing. It's a good feeling to be needed by someone, Dunya, especially when you love that person the way I adore your Mom. She's like a sister to me, a sister who I happen to work for." And that is Alice. Lovely, loving Alice.

And here we are, Mama and me, playing cards. The rules are easy, but she wins all five rounds. Okay, I let her win two of them, but only two. Mama asks Alice to play some music. Philippe Rombi's *Une Hirondelle A Fait Le Printemps*. I have no idea what the title means: I never got around to checking the translation, but the entire song is music without lyrics, and it is soothing, and Mama likes to listen to songs on repeat.

Being with Mama reminds me of my life before my marriage. This house brings back so many childhood memories. My brother, Yasser, who is two years older than me, was always out somewhere playing soccer (or *football* depending on where you are from—we are quite influenced by America here, so we say soccer, although older generations call it football since we were once under a British protectorate). He barely gave me attention. But when I turned eighteen, we became close. He was becoming more open about his sexuality. And we jokingly referred to ourselves, along with Alia, as three sisters. I taught him how to apply mascara, and we would spend hours listening to music together in his room. We shared the same taste in Broadway music, which was odd since most people our age were listening to hip-hop and electro-pop.

My sister Alia is a year younger than me, and we were always close. There was no sibling rivalry, no tension, no tattling on each other. Alia and I were not allowed to go out much, so we spent a lot of time indoors together. Like Yasser, she had a lot of friends, and she knew I liked my privacy, so she never asked me to join her, but always insisted I was free to do so if I changed my mind. I never did. I, the introvert, read and wrote instead. But I was never bored. I did not understand boredom in those days. Though I was a girl and was encouraged to stay home, I never felt left out or complained that the world was unjust. I liked being at home. It was only when I got married that I starting focusing more on the injustice against women. It was only when I got married that I first started feeling bored. I hated it when Adam was at work. I never knew what to do. And though I visited Layla often, and though I still read and wrote, boredom and I became close acquaintances.

IT IS 8:00 p.m. I have been at Mama's all day, but I do not want to leave. I pick up the phone to tell Adam that Mom and I are about to watch a movie and I have decided to spend the night here. "Oh," I hear him say. Why does he sound irritated? I ask if he minds me sleeping over here, and he says, "Of course not, of course not. Enjoy yourself. See you tomorrow."

I do not sleep in my room. I sleep in Mama's room. It is a king-sized bed, but even though I am not cuddled beside her, I feel close to her. I wake up in the middle of the night, sobbing. Mama wiggles her body to reach mine and squeezes my hand.

"Sleep, my child, sleep. Everything is okay now. Sleep, my baby. Sleep."

And I do.

I WAKE up early and ask Alia to drop me home after having breakfast with Mom. I call Adam as soon as I get home. He is at work. I tell him I am going to see Dr. Zahra, and he says my appointment is in three days.

"Yes, I know," I say, "but I messaged her earlier for an emergency meeting." He asks me what is wrong, and I tell him I do not know, I feel depressed again and need to see her.

"Okay," he says, "update me."

FACING THE middle-aged supermodel, Dr. Zahra, I already feel better. Not because she is aesthetically pleasing (I have seen the way people ogle her when she drops me to the elevator), but because I love being around her. I can never get enough of her. Just being in her presence improves my state of mind. I swear it has nothing to do with her looks. I love her personality. She is a qualified therapist, and she saved me from myself. I feel relaxed because I know Dr. Zahra will figure out why I am so sad. And I know that no matter what awaits me when I leave her office, in this hour with her, I am in good hands.

I tell her I do not know why I am so depressed after seeing Mama last night. Should I not be happy? Should I not be ecstatic?

"It may have been too sudden, too overwhelming for you. Even though you consciously wanted to see her, maybe you weren't subconsciously prepared." Dr. Zahra is wearing a yellow skirt, a crisp white shirt, and black heels with red soles. She is writing something in her notebook.

"Dunya?" I look up. She is waiting for me to say something.

"Yes," I say because that seems to be the appropriate answer when someone says your name, right?

"I don't want to administer pills to you again. We have successfully managed to wean you off them, but I think we should increase our appointments to twice a week for a month, and if you still have bouts of depression, we may have to get you back on the pills. How does that sound to you?"

I tell her that sounds good. But it does not sound good to me at all. I worry that it is unhealthy to go on and off pills. But I trust Dr. Zahra. I do not want the pills. But I would rather take them than deal with this depression. Will it keep creeping up on me like this? I do not want to go home to Adam. I want to stay in Dr. Zahra's office all day. And, strangely, I do not want to see Mama for a while. What is wrong with me? Dr. Zahra is right. Maybe I am overwhelmed. These feelings are bound to subside soon.

ON THE way back home, I wish I had not driven to Dr. Zahra's office. On days like this, when I am feeling fragile, I should wait until Adam is home to make an appointment so he can drive me. I feel nauseated. Home is fifteen minutes away. I can do this. "Breathe. Breathe," I tell myself. "Keep driving and breathe." I cannot. No, I cannot do this. My rib muscles seem to be pressing against my lungs. That is not possible, is it? I remind myself it is just anxiety. There is nothing physically wrong with me. But I cannot drive.

I put the flashers on and park to the side of the road and turn the engine off. *Just ten more minutes left to get home*, I tell myself. I roll the windows down, start the car again and get back on the road. And I continue driving. How many more minutes? Five. "Keep going, Dunya," I hear the chorus say. "Keep going."

I want people to see what they have done to me, how they have judged me, and how they have abandoned me. How they have made me mentally and physically sick. I want to write an open thank you letter to those who love me. I want to tell Mama how ill I am feeling. But I also want her to know how happy I am she is back in life. I remember how hurt I felt when Alia told me Mama was ready to see me. Ready? It felt like an insult. But maybe I was not ready to see her. Maybe now it is my turn to wait until I am ready. Maybe my upset stomach was trying to tell me something. I must learn to attune to my body. Maybe what I feel is residual anger. Maybe I am angry that Mama thinks she can just come back into my life as though nothing had happened. There is no hiding it. I am filled with rage. Where was this anger when Alia told me Mama wanted to see me or when I was eating my favorite dishes at Mama's house or while I was playing cards with her? Two minutes left. I am on the road where I live with Adam. Breathe and keep driving. Oh, my chest. One more minute. Here is the house. I have arrived. Oh, thank God. I park the car, turn off the engine, get out of the car, lock it, and tread wearily toward the entrance. I am about to take the keys of the house out of my purse when the door opens.

It is Adam. "I left work early," he says. "I was worried about you. Your cell phone is switched off."

"No, it's not," I say. I take my phone out of my bag to show him, but the battery is dead. "Oops, sorry," I say. I remember Alice's words. *It's good to feel needed by someone you love.* And I want to agree with her. But strangely at this moment, I feel annoyed by Adam. How creepy that he left work to check on me. I am not a child. What is happening to me? I usually love Adam's attention. I feel like throwing up. I hate him. I hate everyone right now, including Mama. Everyone but Layla and Dr. Zahra. Oh no, I am slipping away, am I not?

WHEN THE HABOOB SINGS

Adam and I walk inside the house. Once we are inside our bedroom, facing one another on the edge of the bed, he leans forward and hugs me, but I am motionless, and my arms are limp. I cannot move. I cannot hug him. My eyes are welling up. He pulls back and looks me in the face, a look of concern. He asks me what happened. I tell him nothing happened, everything was fine until this morning. I feel depressed and angry and want to be left alone. Instead of respecting my wish for space, he follows me to the bathroom. I do not have the energy to take a shower, but I splash my face with cold water. Adam hands me a hand towel. I walk back to the bedroom and open the cupboard. I take off my clothes, throw them on the floor, put on sweatpants and a T-shirt and get into bed. Adam picks up my clothes and folds them. I ask him to throw them in the hamper. I fluff up my pillow and lay my head on it. I close my eyes and open them again after a few moments. Adam comes close to me. He is kissing my neck. Oh, he is breathing loudly. And now he is moaning. I jolt out of bed.

"Don't touch me! Are you sick? I am feeling terrible, and you want to make a move on me? Get out of my sight, you pervert! Leave!" I throw the blanket off me, lean toward the bedside lamp, unplug it, and fling it across on the floor, not aiming at him, of course. I hear the bulb shatter. Adam mutters something about me being sick, crazy, and leaves the room, slamming the door. I get out of bed, bend down, caress a shard of glass, and pierce my left wrist with it. I am just piercing the surface, mind you. I just want to feel something. I promise I do not want to kill myself. You have to believe me. And it is only one wrist. I did not cut the other one. That speaks volumes, right? I am fine. Am I not?

I am shouting: *Adam! Adam!* He comes running back into the room. He has that look again, the terrified one, but there are no nurses around us this time. He has to handle this alone, and from the look on his face I do not know if he can. Blood is gushing, spurting out. He is holding the open wound, sobbing. I am wailing. He carries me and takes me to the living room. He commands me not to move. I cannot even if I want to. I have no energy and I am terrified. He rushes to the bathroom and comes back with a bandage. He ties it around my wrist. I feel a burning pain. Why is my hand burning? Oh, the pain is too much to bear! But I do not know whether it is physical or emotional pain that hurts more. And the chorus says, "Both, Dunya! Both!"

I am watching my husband as he speaks frantically on the phone. He is asking for an ambulance. I hope they come in time. Am I going to die?

I HEAR the wail of sirens, finally, after what seems like eons. Two men come in. They remind me of the good cop and the bad cop from movies. One is in a foul mood. The chorus whispers to me that it is because he would rather be treating real cases, not cases such as mine: self-inflicted, selfish. The other man is kind: he assures me that everything is fine, the cut, thankfully, is not too deep. He adds a bandage over the one I have on and applies pressure. I wince. When he tells me to relax, the chorus joins in, telling me I am going to be fine, not to worry, then adding I may just die.

Oddly, neither of the paramedics asks me what happened. Do they know? Is this common? I am not ashamed, I am afraid. Yes, afraid. I will admit it: I am afraid I have no control over myself. First the pills, and now this?

In the ambulance now, Adam is holding my hand. I am wearing an oxygen mask. Why do I need oxygen? But I am too tired to ask. The man in the good mood is driving the ambulance, and the other paramedic, who was in a foul mood earlier, is sitting beside me, no longer scowling. He checks my blood pressure. And now he is holding my hand, telling me not to worry, everything will be okay. I try to lift my head, but it is heavy.

IN THE hospital bed, I beg Adam not to tell anyone what I have done. He still has that concerned look on his face. The doctor approaches and tells me I will not need stitches, but this incident has to be investigated. He asks me what happened, but I cannot answer. He looks at my husband, who is slouched, looking at the ground, shuffling his feet.

When the doctor leaves, Adam says: "If you don't tell them, I will. You need serious help."

"Please, Adam. I can't go back to that psychiatric retreat again. I beg you. I don't even know why it's called a retreat. Oh, please, Adam. You're my cure, please."

"Your *cure*, Dunya? You shouted at me! You called me a pervert for trying to be intimate with you. I'm your husband. But forget all that. It's my fault. Wrong timing. I can admit that. But, what came over you afterward? You tried to kill yourself again. I thought we were done with all that. I thought the therapy was working."

"It *is* working. I am better. I don't know what happened."

"See that's what scares me. It's like this sudden thing. You don't even know you're going to do it. You have no control over yourself. It was the exact same thing with the pills. I thought that was a one-off. Oh no..." He is shaking his head.

"Adam, please. Please don't tell anyone what happened. Don't tell the doctors. Don't tell Mama."

"I have to say something if you won't. I can't live with this kind of responsibility. If you try this again and die, it's on my conscience."

How can I convince him not to say anything?

"I didn't want to kill myself, Adam. Cutting my wrist isn't killing myself. I only cut one wrist, baby. You heard the ambulance driver. He said the cut was not too deep, and the doctor says I don't need stitches."

"But what if you had hit a vein?"

I want to tell him: Please no what-ifs. Please, let us forget this. But I cannot speak. I want to vow this will never happen again. But how do I know if it will or will not? What if he is right? What if I have no control over myself? Am I going to kill myself accidentally one day? Do I need to be admitted for the rest of my life? Am I on suicide watch again?

Adam is waiting for an answer. I hold his hand. He pulls it away from me.

"How can I leave you alone and go to work? I can't do this. I can't make sure you're okay all the time."

"You're leaving me?"

"I'm not leaving, D. I'm right here. But I mean I don't think it's safe for you to come back home with me. At least in a ward, in that retreat you were in before, they'll take care of you."

"I don't want to go there again." I have tears in my eyes, but I do not want to cry. I do not want him to see how feeble I am.

"You know what? I don't get it. You're supposed to be happy. You're out of jail, you're resolving things with your family. You and I were doing well. I thought you let go of all that. Why can't you just let go?"

Let go of what? I want to ask Adam. Let go of my Baba's death, Adam? Is that what I should let go of? Let go of Mama coming back into my life when she was *ready*? Let go of going back to Mama when I was not? Let go of Alia who insinuated she got in touch with me because her boyfriend Jeremy was pestering her to? Let go of the fact that my brother still does not talk to me? Let go of the fact that I have no control over this inner desire to hurt myself? I want to ask him all these questions aloud, but instead, I look up at him, waiting for him to say something so I do not have to answer.

"Dunya, say something. What's going on inside your head? How do I know you won't try to kill yourself again? Dammit. I can't deal with this."

"I swear it won't happen again. I wanted to punish you, to punish everyone, to punish myself. But I swear I didn't want to kill myself. I had just had an emergency meeting with Dr. Zahra, and you wanted to touch me."

"I'm sorry I repulsed you so much that you felt like killing yourself."

Why does he keep saying I want to kill myself? Did I want to die? And I find myself saying something I do not mean, something I never thought I would say or think. Maybe I am crazy. Maybe I have no control over myself. Maybe I am under the spell of a dictator in my head. Maybe I do need help. I say: "If you need physical relations with someone, please go ahead. It's not cheating if I suggest it. Don't tell me about it though."

"Where did that come from? You're disturbed, D. This is too much. I can't believe you just said that." He has tears in his eyes. "I could never do that. If I wanted that kind of lifestyle, I would have never gotten married. And for you to be okay with me doing that hurts. I can't believe you could be so heartless."

"Oh, I'm so sorry, Adam. I didn't mean it. And I'm sorry for having rejected you. I can't apologize enough. I just felt numb. I *feel* numb. I was so overwhelmed after seeing Mama. I just wanted to be alone. I love you so much, Adam. I hope you understand."

"I understand." And I can tell from his eyes he does. Yes, my beloved Adam understands. What a good man I have.

"Wait a minute," the chorus hisses, "Adam is not such a good man. He wanted to leave you when you came out of jail and how selfish he is to have wanted to touch you when you clearly needed space. No, he's not that good of a man. Watch out, Dunya. Watch out!"

I tell the chorus to be quiet.

"Stay awake, Dunya," the chorus warns me, ignoring my attempts to silence it. "Stay awake, or you'll wake up in the psychiatric ward. Don't sleep. They'll take you away from here. Don't sleep. Don't sleep..."

I WAKE up. I look around to make sure I am still in the hospital ward. Thankfully, I am. I cannot live in this fear. Where is Adam? Will he tell them? No, he cannot. He will not.

Oh God, where are you? Give me a sign, God. Oh, make me better, God. Why the mystery, God? Why can't you present yourself to me? I love you so much, God. Love me in return. Oh, love me in return! Oh, for peace, God! Oh, for your love!

The prayer works. I swear it does. Prayer has always worked for me. I feel calm. There is something about talking to God that has always soothed me.

I need to change my life. I need to, as Adam insists, let go. How can I when I have no control? I remember picking up the shard and not thinking twice about hurting myself. I promise to myself that I will be more mindful from now on. I cannot control my depression right now, but I can focus all my energy on making sure I do not hurt myself. I do not want to go to a psychiatric retreat. I will call Dr. Zahra tomorrow and tell her to come to the hospital and I will turn my life around. I promise. But am I lying to myself? Maybe I will never recover and my life will be a series of admittances and discharges from hospitals wards and psychiatric retreats until someone decides to lock me up for good in a mental institution. Is psychiatric retreat a euphemism for mental institution? It must be. I am sure there is no difference. Bars on the window. Locked up. Is using the phrase mental institution politically correct? Who cares? I am the crazy one. And I, the crazy one, am not offended.

What happened to me? Why did I have a relapse? And the chorus suggests that it may not have been a relapse, that I was mad all along.

I MUST have fallen asleep when Adam told them. Because when I wake up, I am no longer in the hospital, but back in the psychiatric ward.

It is the same bed in the same room with the same dreary view. They might as well reserve the room for me. The tiles on the wall are cobalt blue and the floor tiles (some of which are cracked) are white. Maybe my powers of observation are getting better because my mind wants to distract me from the monsters lurking inside the caverns of my mind. But wait a minute... I was better off when I was self-engrossed. Or maybe I was not? Was I ever normal? And what is normal? Is Earth not just one big mental asylum? Are we not just on varying ends of the insanity spectrum? I look closer at the cobalt blue tiles. Why are there tiles on the wall in the first place? They call this a retreat? I feel as though I am in a bathroom. They should not have tiles on the wall. No. They should have normal walls. Normal. That word again. They should have painted the normal walls yellow. I heard that yellow makes people happy, and I would do anything to be happy.

Even being in a cell feels better than being in this place. I should not be here. All the reasons for my depression are justified: a dead father, a mother and sister who are back in my life after leaving me when I needed them most, and a brother who would rather spend time with his boyfriend than take care of his unstable sister. Oh, and a husband who has had me admitted without my consent.

Here comes the chorus: "You brought this onto yourself. You are the creator of this mess. Stop blaming others. *You* wrote the article. *You* cut yourself. What did you expect? That your husband would risk that happening again? And *you* took those pills. There's nobody to blame but yourself. If everyone collapsed when challenging things started happening to them, the whole world would be locked up. But most people are out there. And you are in here. So stop acting as though your breakdown is warranted."

Let me explain this more clearly. When I took those pills, I know I should have stopped. But I did not want to. That does not mean I *could not* stop, right? And it is the same with the shard of glass. I did not want to kill myself. I could have stopped, but I did not *want* to. But could I have stopped? Am I making any sense? Who am I fooling? It happened so fast I could not have stopped.

A lot of people want to do dangerous things but do not do them. I did. Maybe I should not be angry that I am in here. I cut my wrist. And that is not normal behavior. Is this a good sign? That I am admitting that it was not normal? Oh, I am tired again.

But as I am drifting off to sleep, the chorus asks me a question that I cannot answer, at least not just yet. It asks: "Are you alive or dead, Dunya? Are you alive or dead?"

What a terrifying prospect! Am I alive? I pinch myself. I begin to scratch my forearms, but stop myself, because if the nurses see any marks, they will keep me in here for longer. I have to act like I am okay so I can get out of here fast. I pinch my skin again softly and am unsure whether I am alive. And if I am dead, when did I die? In the cell? When I took those pills? When I cut myself? As I rattle my brain trying to think of when I could have died, the chorus commands me to sleep.

And I obey, eyelids heavy.

THE NURSE is opening the curtains. The sun is blinding. I squint. I tell Nurse Leah it is too bright in here. She tells me my eyes will adjust in a few moments. A maid brings breakfast to my bed. An orange. Apple juice. Pancakes. Honey on the side. Two slices of toast. There are those little plastic containers of butter and jam. I check to see if it is strawberry jam. No. Apricot. There is also a bowl of yogurt. I am not hungry, but I want to coat my stomach so they can give me pills and I can pass out again. The maid asks if I need anything else. "No, thank you," I reply. The nurse is waiting beside my bed with a plastic cup filled with pills. Is this their idea of treatment, keeping me passed out all day? Without intending to I have asked this question aloud.

"Only because it's a weekend. There are no psychiatrists here, so they want to keep you sedated. They will see you tomorrow when they are back," the nurse says, smiling.

So, to them, sedated means safe, it means my chances of having a breakdown are unlikely. I do not want to see any doctors. I want to see Dr. Zahra.

"Can I call my psychiatrist?" I ask.

"It's not allowed right now. You can ask the doctors tomorrow. You can call your husband if you want though."

"What a strange rule. I'm not allowed to call a psychiatrist in a psychiatric retreat, but I can call my family?"

"Only today, ma'am. Once the doctors are back the rules will change. Today you can call your husband."

I do not believe her. I think she is making up the rules as she goes along to justify her stupidity for telling me I cannot call a psychiatrist. I have no energy to confront her. And I do not want to take out my anger at Adam on her.

"No way. I don't want to speak to him." The traitor.

"Well, if you want to call your parents, that's fine, too," she says.

My father is dead, I want to say. But I refrain. "Yes, I'd like to call my mother," I lie.

"Now?"

"Yes, please. What's your name?"

"Leah."

"Shall we go now, Nurse Leah?"

She tells me to eat my breakfast first so she can administer my pills. I make myself a butter and apricot jam sandwich and drink the apple juice. I tell her I cannot eat anything else, and I devour the pills she holds out for me. I drag myself out of bed, walk to the bathroom, brush my teeth, wash my face, and walk outside my room to where Nurse Leah is waiting for me. I already feel lethargic but I have to make the call to Dr. Zahra.

We walk down the hall to the elevator, and inside the lift, Nurse Leah presses the ground floor. The doors open. She leads me to an office. There is a sign outside the door: *Personnel*. She tells me to dial 9 before the number. I have ten minutes to speak with my mother. "Thank you," I whisper. I ask if I can speak to my mom privately. She nods, walks toward the door, opens it, and closes it behind her. Then she comes back and tells me I have ten minutes. She adds that the pills may begin to work, and she wants to make sure I am able to walk properly back to my room before they really kick in.

I dial Dr. Zahra's number. My eyelids are heavy. The room is spinning. She answers on the second ring. I tell her I have been hospitalized again and am supposed to be calling my mother, I need to see her, I am okay because of the pills, but I still feel like I am losing control. "Calm down," she says. I wish I could tell her that whenever anyone tells me to calm down, it has the opposite effect on me. I tend to freak out instead. But the pills seem to be taking an effect on me. Not quite though. My mind is still hyperactive. I remember the exercise she taught me for when I feel overwhelmed, and though I do not feel overwhelmed, I count sounds and identify visuals. Sound one: her voice, telling me she will come to visit me today, she has authorization. Sound two: my voice telling her not to mention to the nurse that I called her, to say that I told my mother to call her after speaking with me and to inform her where I was. Sound three: footsteps in the hall. Visual one: a painting of an Arabic coffee jug. Visual two: a sofa, beige, with two white cushions. Sound four: Nurse Leah tapping gently on the door. That was not ten minutes. No way! Visual three: an unlit battery-operated candle on a desk. Sound five: me saying goodbye to Dr. Zahra. And sound six: the tone on the phone as the line goes dead. Sound seven: Nurse Leah knocking more loudly now. Sound eight: me saying: "Come in."

I walk back to my room. Nurse Leah is holding me as I succumb to drowsiness. The good thing about the pills is that the darkness cannot stick. My mind becomes slippery, both racy and still. I know the darkness is trying to creep like ivy up the recesses of my psyche. But the pills, ah yes, the pills: they stand guard, shooing the darkness away, telling it that it is not welcome. And the darkness smirks, warning menacingly that it will find a way. It will keep pushing, it insists, until I need stronger and stronger pills. It will not rest until I lay embryonic on the floor, never again to rise from the ashes of despair.

Nurse Leah asks me if I would like to sit in the courtyard. What an idiotic question! She administered sedatives to me and now thinks I have the energy to sit in a courtyard? I tell her I am tired. I ask her why I never see any patients. She tells me most of the patients are on the upper floors. Why am I alone on this floor? I ask. She tells me that this floor is reserved for VIPs. I am a VIP? Me? How odd! Why? Because I write? Yes, ma'am. Because you are a famous writer and the doctor at the hospital advised us to keep you in seclusion in case... Ah yes, in case someone wants to beat me up. Not to that extreme, ma'am. I want to tell her to stop calling me ma'am but I realize I refer to her as Nurse Leah or Nurse. So, ma'am it is.

We are in my room now. I tuck myself in bed and cover my face with the starchy sheets. *Come quickly,*

Dr. Zahra, I think. *Come quickly.* The nurse turns off the light and closes the curtains. She walks toward me and puts her hand on my forehead and keeps it there for a few moments. I remember my mother. I ask Nurse Leah if I have a fever. No, she replies. Her hand is now stroking my hair. Oh, how I need to be touched. I sink into the bed as Nurse Leah connects with me through her hands, letting me know that she is here for me without saying a word. I ask her to hug me. She sits on my bed and holds my head to her bosom, pats the back of my head, rocking me back and forth, back and forth. She is good at this nurturing thing. I want to cry, but those pills...

    I say thank you. My speech is slurred, and my vision is blurred. I want to confess to her that I called Dr. Zahra, that I feel guilty, but the chorus shuts me up. It tells me not to upset Nurse. But nothing can upset Nurse Leah, I say to the chorus. She likes me. I feel it.

    And now the chorus, or is it Nurse Leah, is singing a one-word lullaby: *Sleep. Sleep. Sleep. Sleep.*

I WAKE up to Nurse Leah tapping me gently. "Dunya, Dunya..."

I keep my eyes closed. Maybe if I ignore her she will go away. The pills must have worn off because my mind is racing. What time is it? Did Dr. Zahra already come and leave?

"Dunya," Nurse Leah continues, tapping my hand. "I just got a call from reception. There is a doctor here to see you. She's waiting in an office upstairs."

I open my eyes and jolt out of bed. "Dr. Zahra?"

"Yes. How do you know?" Her eyebrows are raised.

My mind scrambles to recall the excuse I gave Dr. Zahra on the phone earlier. "Um, well. Uh. When I spoke to my mother earlier, I told her to tell Dr. Zahra where I was." I look at Nurse Leah. She is smiling. Phew. I notice crow's feet around the corners of her eyes. And deep furrowed lines across her forehead. She looks too young to have wrinkles. I wonder how old she is. Is it rude to ask?

"Well, come on, Dunya, you can see her now."

"Nurse?"

"Yes?"

"How old are you?"

WHEN THE HABOOB SINGS

"Why are you asking, dear?" She is blushing. I should not have asked. I have made her nervous. Or maybe she is socially awkward like I am and blushes when someone asks a question, any question.

"I don't know. I guess I'm just curious." I look away to avoid her gaze. And then turn to look at her again.

"Is my age important ma'am?" She raises an eyebrow.

"No." But it is more important than ever now that she has shrouded her age in mystery.

"In that case, forget you asked. Let's go quickly. The doctor is waiting."

I walk to the bathroom, wash my face, and brush my teeth again. I come out of the bathroom and let Nurse Leah guide me to an office on the fifth floor.

DR. ZAHRA is sitting behind a desk. She greets Nurse Leah and gestures for me to sit on the chair facing her. She looks concerned. Do medical experts have no idea how essential it is to always wear a poker face with anxious people? When Dr. Zahra in particular is concerned, which is extremely rare, I panic. I hear my stomach rumble. I am about to pick at my cuticles, but I stop myself. I need to breathe deeply. Inhale. Exhale. Inhale, yes good girl. Exhale, yes. Instead of relaxing, my breath becomes shallower. I will myself to catch my breath. I need to convince Dr. Zahra I will be fine, that I *am* fine. I need to hear her tell me everything is going to be okay. Nurse Leah tells us we can stay in the office for as long as we need and walks out of the room.

"So, tell me what happened." She looks at me for a few moments, too long for my liking, and perhaps noticing this, being as intuitive as she is, she looks away. Or maybe she looks away because I admitted to her once that I do not like prolonged eye contact.

"I hope you will believe me when I say I didn't want to kill myself. I just wanted to cut my wrists. Well, actually just one wrist. Even the doctor said it wasn't a deep cut."

"What you have to understand is that cutting your wrists—or wrist—is dangerous." Oh no, she is using a new tone of voice, the kind a mother uses on a child, a very naughty child. Have we regressed? Have I regressed? "If you want to hurt yourself that badly, who knows what else you are capable of? It might start out superficially, and eventually, as you grow accustomed to the pain, you may cut deeper and deeper. You said you were not intending to take all those pills, but you ended up overdosing. This is risky behavior. You are now on suicide watch. Your nurse has informed me they don't even keep pills on your tray. When she's sure you have swallowed them, she can leave. And no, in case you're wondering, that's not the case with all the patients here. The concern is that you might save the pills and take them all at once after a few days."

I am flabbergasted. "No. That thought never once crossed my mind. Oh, please don't think that, Dr. Zahra." I pick at my cuticles.

"I am here to make sure you won't harm yourself again." She walks toward me and sits on the chair beside me. "You were not able to control your urge to cut yourself, and that is dangerous in and of itself." Why is she repeating how dangerous it is? I got it.

Oh no, does she agree that I should be in here? She is my rope of freedom, and I feel her slipping away from my grip. I want to hold her and beg her not to leave me here, but I compose myself. Maybe if I pretend hard enough, I will not pose a danger to myself.

"Okay Dr. Zahra, I'll admit I don't feel okay. But I can pretend to. Isn't that what the whole world is doing?

Pretending? I got this. I do. I can pretend and get on with my life until I'm better."

"What's important is to feel good on the inside, Dunya. When you feel good within yourself, there is no need to pretend."

"Can you get me out of here?" I ask, eyes brimming with tears. I want her to hold me and take me home. Maybe if I live with her for a few weeks, I will recover sooner. Yes, that is a radical form of therapy but I can guarantee it will work. I do not have the nerve to tell her.

"I can, and I will, but let me tell you this, Dunya. I understand what you are going through, but you are in too much of a rush to be okay. This is why you collapsed after meeting your mother. You never addressed what you were feeling. I explained this to you, how you were overwhelmed. You still are overwhelmed. I have faith in you. But you need to give yourself time. You've had a lot of situations that warrant a breakdown, such as your arrest and your father's death. And all your family issues with your mom and siblings. But how you choose to respond to the breakdown is the key to your freedom. And even in your case, which may appear to be a challenging one to yourself and others, it is a choice, whether you acknowledge that right or don't. When you lose the gift of choice, you lose yourself in the process. You can try by practicing mindfulness, being in the moment, registering every emotion. I know you can recover. But give yourself time. My advice right now is not to think of this place as a psychiatric retreat. Instead, think of it as a resort. It's not a bad place. It's different from other psychiatric centers locally.

WHEN THE HABOOB SINGS

That's why it's called a retreat. There is a beautiful courtyard, a swimming pool, a gym. Enjoy yourself."

"I don't feel like exercising." I pout. Maybe if she sees how sad I am she can sign a release form right away. She is right. I have a choice to get better. It is simple. If she believes I have a choice, why am I still confined in here? Time, the chorus sings, time.

"You don't have to exercise. But it's nice to know these amenities are here, isn't it? Maybe you can check them out. Think of it as a five-star resort version of a psychiatric retreat."

"Well, my view sucks. And the room is ugly. It looks like a bathroom."

Dr. Zahra chuckles. I love her laugh.

"Do you know there are stables? You can even go horse-riding if you want."

"I don't know how to."

"You can learn, dear. Look, if you aren't ready to explore the facilities, at least you have the luxury of sleeping when you want, you get to be away from people, and you can write. This is a good time to think about everything that has happened, to take note of your anger, your feelings of being betrayed, your grief, even your shock. Write everything down. If you want, I can bring you a notebook and a pen when I come to see you tomorrow or I can tell the nurse to give you a notebook now." I look at her fingernails, painted a crimson red. She is so immaculate.

Dr. Zahra takes out her cell phone and reading glasses. She looks at her phone and tells me she has to get home. Her husband is waiting for her. It is the first time she mentions her husband. I have noticed her wedding band before, but she has never spoken about her personal life and I never asked. I wonder if she has children. She peers at me from behind her reading glasses. She takes them off and places them back in her handbag.

"Well? Shall I tell the nurse to get you something to write on today?"

"No, I want a notebook from you. You're coming to see me again tomorrow, right?" I ask, voice cracking. I know I sound desperate, but I need Dr. Zahra.

"Yes," she says. "The doctors will be making the rounds tomorrow, so I will join them."

"Oh please, yes! I need you here."

"You don't need me, Dunya. You don't need anyone. You are more independent than you think. And you're strong, much more than you know. Give yourself credit. And keep reminding yourself that you have a choice to take care of yourself. It's a choice and not a struggle. Okay? Many people admire you, but what you need most right now is to admire yourself. All I need from you is a commitment to loving and accepting yourself, to getting better. Are you committed to that? Deal?" She extends her hand to shake mine.

I tell her my cuticles are bleeding, so I cannot shake her hand. Dr. Zahra laughs and reaches over to hug me. She smells of rosewater and incense. I wish she would never let me go.

Yes, I tell myself. Deal. Done. I am committed. Committed to getting better, and as the chorus reminds me, committed in this prison, this mental asylum. I will try not to see this place as a psychiatric retreat, but as a resort. So many times in my life, I have wanted to escape to a place and travel alone. I was never allowed, being a girl and all. I am not lamenting, I was happy growing up. I want to be happy again, and I will commit myself to being happy again. But what if it was never happiness? What if I was in a bubble sheltered away from reality? What if this was reality? This grief, this pain, this sadness, this fear. What if this is the truth and my previous carefree life was a lie, an illusion. But even with all the pain, sadness, grief, and fear, an unexpected guest always appears when I am in Dr. Zahra's presence. And that guest is hope. Dr. Zahra gives me hope. And it is this hope that promises me I will recover. And I can do this. Whatever this is.

I MET the doctors this morning. I have never had a job before, and have never been interviewed, but I can honestly say this is the closest I have ever gotten to an application for anything. In this morning's case, I was applying for sanity. I was not nervous. I had pills inside of me. And Dr. Zahra was there.

Dr. Zahra brought me a notebook as promised. The cover: glossy white with a green teddy bear holding a fluorescent yellow star. Inside: plain blue-lined paper, nothing to write home about. I guess she did not have time to go to a stationery shop. Any gift, no matter how tacky, from Dr. Zahra is worth it.

She told me with a wink that I am world-famous now, so maybe my diary will be compiled into memoirs one day, or someone can write a biography about me using these entries or make a documentary out of my musings.

The doctors decided I would be allowed to have two phone calls a day: one to my husband (who I do not want to speak to for I hate him) and another to my mother (who I cannot speak to for I am too ashamed).

WHEN THE HABOOB SINGS

When the doctors left after interrogating me, Dr. Zahra said she thought I should call my husband. I tell her I am not ready for it yet. She nodded and left.

I AM lying in bed. I am going to try this diary thing.

Dear Diary,

I met the doctors today. And I, the anxious one who gets nervous when I'm being looked at, was too sedated to feel nervous. Dr. Zahra filled them in on my situation. There were four of them apart from her. There was a religious psychiatrist with a frizzy beard, who recommended a pilgrimage to Mecca and more pills. He was wearing a traditional white robe but no headgear. He didn't seem too happy with me, telling me I am facing a spiritual crisis and that by shattering my Islamic foundation, I have placed myself on shaky ground. He assures me that if I return to the faith, I will feel stable in no time. I wasn't offended. I understood where he was coming from. His whole life is built on faith, and he sincerely believes in what he is saying. And I liked him. Beneath his rigid demeanor, there was something about him that felt calming. Is this what they call good vibes? Well, that is what I got around him: good vibes, although I had the urge to trim his beard, or at least recommend a good conditioner for it. Or a frizz serum.

Anyway, this religious doctor seemed intent on helping me albeit in an unscientific manner. Maybe he was telling me to return to the faith for rewards in the afterlife. Who knows? Anyway, I liked him. Yes, I liked him a lot. He didn't have to come today, or if he had to, he could've just stayed quiet, but he did his job, in the only way he knew how, as a medical practitioner-cum-spiritual therapist. He was the consummate professional.

There was another young lady who looked too young to be a professional, consummate or otherwise. Good genes, perhaps. She was soft-spoken, and though she was unveiled and wearing a body-hugging dress with her cleavage showing, she agreed with the religious doctor. She explained that religion is a part of our identity and it shapes our lives. So when we leave it, grief is inevitable because our spiritual foundation, an important part of our sense of security, crashes. In short, her analysis was that losing my faith, compounded with the grief I faced with Baba's death, led to my nervous breakdown. She told me Dad wouldn't come back (is that not stating the obvious, doc?), but I always had access to the faith. She gave me a pamphlet to read. I looked at it: *Islam, the religion of peace*. And she gave me a small Koran, which is something I would have expected the bearded psychiatrist to do, not this young lady in her provocative dress. But I guess we should never judge a book by its cover, huh? Which reminds of the green teddy bear with the fluorescent star. Ha!

The other doctor, another young man—at what age are they graduating these days?—told me to follow my truth. The religious man glared at him, but he continued, saying that what will make me happy is authenticity. He said that in time, as I adjust to the whirlwind that has become my life, I will find peace. He also added that it was the death threats, the judgment by our society, my father's death, and my family's abandonment that were the catalysts for my breakdown. Needless to say, I liked his opinion best. The fourth doctor told me that I have repressed all my emotions, tucked them away in the recesses of my subconscious and as a result, all the repressive thoughts have now erupted like a volcano into my consciousness. This is Post-Traumatic Stress Disorder, she adds. She suggests writing affirmations in my diary and observations of what I am learning.

And Dr. Zahra nodded a lot adding that staying here would be the best thing for me. I guess she didn't have to say much. She is my therapist. We have plenty of time to discuss matters alone.

Dear Diary,

Today was so boring. Boring, boring, boring. I woke up, had breakfast and took a shower. I went back to sleep, woke up had lunch, went back to sleep, woke up again, went to the courtyard for a walk, came back to my room, took another shower, and had dinner. And now I am going to sleep again! So boring. I asked Nurse Leah why nobody was in the courtyard, and she said some of the patients were horse-riding and the others were swimming. I went to visit the swimming pool. There were four girls there, young ladies. Do you know what broke my heart? They all looked normal. But normal is relative, right diary? Anyway, one was doing the backstroke, two were playing volleyball in the pool with a beach-ball. And one of them was reading a book. I got closer to have a look at the title but she began screaming loudly until Nurse Leah dragged me away. So much for normal. I asked Nurse what was wrong with her and she said it is confidential.

I cannot believe I am in here, all because of an article. People think of apostates as enemies, but they aren't. I'm a testament to that. I'm a simple girl. I miss the sound of the call to prayer in here. There is a prayer room downstairs but, for obvious reasons, I do not go there. But I still love the moment when the Imam calls everyone to prayer in the outside world, bellowing *God is great*. Yes, indeed, God *is* great.

I always loved Ramadan growing up. Though I had only tried fasting a couple of times when I was an early teen, I remember what most of our conversations revolved around in Ramadan. I remembered how at the time of breaking our fast, we would discuss how easy or difficult it was to fast on that day, whether or not we felt thirsty or dizzy or how a date is the best way to break a fast, how we should not eat a salty meal prior to commencing our fast; and why yogurt and rice is the best way to start the day.

Ramadan is such a peaceful month. According to the prophet Mohammed, the devils are locked up during the entire month, so any evil you see is from the ego alone and cannot be blamed on the devil. So what about suicide bombers in Ramadan? How can they be any worse than that throughout the year when the devils are unlocked? What worse can they do when it is not Ramadan and their devils are wild and free?

I am bored. Bored bored bored. I feel like an exotic creature locked up in a zoo while all the other apostates, agnostics, and atheists, my fellow exotic creatures in crime, roam around freely because they are disguised well. I do not know which hurts more: the haters or the silent supporters...

I think the silent supporters hurt more. The ones who have your back but do not want anyone to know. The ones who send private messages because they're too embarrassed or too afraid to write comments supporting you publicly. I have plenty of online silent supporters in my life. And I pity them for their cowardice and hypocrisy. And I pity myself for making them feel embarrassed to be associated with me somehow.

Oh diary, I had a moment of weakness earlier today. I need to write about this. I was looking outside my bedroom window with the bars and I felt nothing. I felt as though I did not exist. I thought about death a lot and I wondered how I could feel such a need to die with all the pills in my system. But I remembered Dr. Zahra's words: I have a choice to take care of myself. And I will grab that choice by its horns, diary. Significant moment, huh? And in that decision, I felt better and even the view transformed. It was not an ugly, barren desert anymore, but a desert brimming with life and possibility. I wonder who lives in that yellow brick compound, diary. I will never find out. Kind of sad, right? Well, whoever lives there, I hope they are happy. I hope they never find out what it is like to be locked up in this place.

Dear Diary,

I wrote an article today! A lengthy one! I will submit it to a newspaper when I'm out of this place. It's about the stigma of mental health. I'm embarrassed to be in here. I know I shouldn't feel ashamed, but I am. I feel crazy. Maybe I am crazy. But maybe I'm not. Either way, I am ashamed. And it's not fair in this day and age that people don't treat mental illness as a serious thing. To be fair, I'm lucky. My husband, who I am still angry at, did treat my depression as a serious thing, so much so that I wish he hadn't, but I'm lucky, yes I am. I acknowledge that now. Most people are told nothing is wrong with them until they are found in an alley somewhere with a syringe dangling out of their arm. Or at home sprawled across the bedroom floor with an empty bottle of vodka, some pills, and a suicide note. In my article, I addressed the majority of people who don't flinch when it comes to depression or anxiety. In our society, most people tell others to pick themselves up and get over it, to be grateful for their bounties. And that is sage advice for someone who is feeling sad, but dangerous when it comes to a depressed person. We don't know the difference. I didn't either until I myself became a victim of depression. No, I'm not a victim. I'm not a victim. I'm NOT a victim.

I wonder if I will be like this forever. Yes, yes, I remember the choice part, but I'm not convinced today. I barely remember what it's like not to be mentally unstable. Maybe it's abnormal *not* to feel depressed. I mean, how can we feel happy on a planet with sex trafficking, childhood prostitution, rape, genocide, war, and pedophilia? How can we feel happy on a planet with racism and ethnic cleansing, persecution, abuse, and violence? I shouldn't carry the weight of the world on my shoulders, I know. But it's not easy living on this planet.

I know I shouldn't concern myself with heavy topics. But these are the topics I want to write about or at least read about. I want to read about what we can do to change all this madness. Maybe we are not treating illnesses in the way we should. There must be another way. Oh, why does life plague me so much? Why can't I just eat, drink, and be merry like so many people on this planet who just go about their day-to-day lives and only feel sad when something happens to them or to their loved ones. What is this lingering pain that won't leave me alone? And why do I think writing about painful topics can alleviate the pain somehow?

Why can't I write beautiful love stories or words that lift people up? I can't change anything, so why have I taken it upon myself to delude myself into thinking I can?

Oh, I'm tired. My mind is tired. Even with the pills that numb me, I am thinking too much. Maybe they have changed the pills. They aren't as powerful. But that's good. It means I am no longer a threat to myself. Right?

Well, back to the article, dearest diary. I want people to know we have to change the way we view depression and anxiety.

WHEN THE HABOOB SINGS

Too many people around the world don't confess to how they are feeling because they are either embarrassed or don't want to burden others. Aren't we supposed to take care of each other? Why do I have to feel ashamed that I am in here? Why do I feel like a burden? Why am I locked up instead of recovering at home with my family cheerleading me from the sidelines?

I know I should call Adam, but I still feel betrayed. I can't call Mama because I wouldn't know what to say.

I don't want to be here. I'm bored. I know Dr. Zahra wants me to see this place as a retreat, but it's not. I don't mind being away from everyone right now. I just don't like the smell here. It smells of hand sanitizer. But I like Nurse Leah. So I can't complain, although her shifts keep changing. The other nurses are nice, too. They occupy my mind. But Nurse Leah inhabits my heart. And the heart is a lofty place.

Maybe I can learn to enjoy this place more. For now, I say good night, diary.

Dear Diary,

I am peaceful
I am happy
I am beautiful
I am peaceful
I am happy
I am beautiful
I am peaceful
I am happy
I am beautiful
I am peaceful
I am happy
I am beautiful

How long does it take for affirmations to work? Or, more importantly, do they even work? I am repeating each of the phrases but crying at the same time. The truth is: I am not peaceful, I am not happy, I am not beautiful, I am not peaceful, I am not happy, and, no, I am certainly not beautiful. I can't lie to you, diary. I feel terrible. And I am so scared, because if this is how depressed I feel with pills, what will happen when I am weaned off them? Or what if I'm kept on them forever this time? I want the pill they gave me when they told me Baba was dead on the day of my release from prison, the one that knocked me out.

Would it be too much to ask them for a stronger sedative? Will they keep me in here longer if I do? Diary, I'm not sharing these entries with anyone. They're way too embarrassing to turn into memoirs or a biography or a documentary about me, even posthumously. Especially posthumously!

Dear Diary,

The chorus has been quite busy lately, one minute telling me that I'm forgotten, the next minute telling me everyone is gossiping about me, and moments later telling me some people with an agenda are using me as an example of what happens to an apostate. But the chorus sometimes shifts gears and tells me how inspiring I am for my society, how courageous I am, what a trailblazer I am, what a pioneer I am. I like being thought of as a trailblazer. I like when the chorus showers me with praise. Is that ego, diary?

Does everyone have a chorus? And is everyone's chorus as schizophrenic as mine? Is our sanity measured by how far we believe our choruses? Some people know how to ignore the voices in their heads. Right? Surely if not, we'd all be holed up in asylums, right? Right? Or is it that some people have peaceful choruses. Can I make mine peaceful ever? Do I really have a choice like Dr. Zahra said? Answer me, diary. Why can't you answer me? What's the point of me writing to you every day when you won't even respond to me?

I hate being me. I hate that I have left religion. I hate that I can't be like so many others, complacent in their beliefs. I hate that I can be the punching bag of religious people when I have not denounced religion publicly in any way. And that is not because I am afraid to denounce religion, but because I have respect for it. Because I know many people around the world find solace in faith whatever their religion. And I love people. Yes, I only have one friend, but that is because I tried making friends but it didn't work out for me, I'm weird, I'm shy and I like to be alone: it is not because I have any kind of aversion toward others. I'm certainly no misanthrope.

Dear Diary,

Dr. Zahra came to visit me in my room today. She says I can leave the day after tomorrow. Oh yes! She asked me about you, diary. She asked if I am writing in you every day. I tell her I am writing *to* you. See the difference? I turned you from an object to *the* object. Anyway, I don't think Dr. Zahra got it. But she was happy that I was writing. Her face beamed! It actually beamed! I made her happy. And that makes me happy in turn.

My mood is lifting, diary. I am not pretending to feel good. I actually do. I have a renewed sense of hope and that's even when Dr. Zahra isn't around. How cool is that? I'm not sure this good feeling will last, but I won't worry about that right now.

WHEN THE HABOOB SINGS

When I told Nurse Leah I feel better and am leaving this place in a couple of days, she cried. She was so happy but said she will miss me. She gave me her number. What a nice lady. She makes me want to become an extrovert.

Dear Diary,

I called Mama today. I didn't want to, but I felt I had to. She was sobbing on the phone. In between sobs, she said I should have called her after the incident. Ah, so cutting my wrist will be referred to as an incident? Mama said Adam has been calling the psychiatric retreat every day since I was admitted to check on my status and to keep her updated. I told her I had needed space, which was the truth, but I left out the part that I am still dealing with residual anger toward her. I know I shouldn't be angry. I mean she lost her husband because of me. Her husband! My father! Yes, I still blame myself for his death and I always will. Maybe I'm not feeling as good as I thought I was yesterday, diary. Oh no. Life is gnawing at me again now that I have to face it once more.

But the guilt is there. It's the truth. A truth that will remain with me. And if I try to let go of the truth, the chorus is there to remind me I am letting go only for me to grasp it tightly once again. When the chorus is in a good mood, it tries to make me feel better by saying that his time had come and that nothing could have changed that. I wish I could believe that, but it's hard under the circumstances. I mean, if it were his time to leave, why couldn't he have died another way? This will always hurt me: the fact that he had a heart attack after trying to see me while I was in prison. Why not in another way? Why?

But I'm not going to bury the pain this time. Mama asked if I was going to ask Adam to pick me up and I told her to send Alia instead. I wasn't ready to speak to him, I explained. Mama said she understood, but I wonder if she really did, diary. I wonder how much of what we say to each other is good old-fashioned bullshit.

After ending our conversation, I felt less angry with Mama. I was still a bit angry but much less. I love her so much. I adore her.

SO HERE we are, I am in the car with Alia on the way to Mama's. She is crying, and I, the sick one, am consoling *her*. She is rambling, saying they all feel so guilty. They should have supported me from the start.

Her phone rings. She checks the screen, and tells me to answer her phone, it is Yasser. I tell her he does not want to speak to me, but she insists that I answer her phone and tells me he is calling for me. "For me?" I ask.

"Yes, answer!"

When I say hello and hear his voice, I burst into tears. I am bawling loudly, and he is bawling now, too. He says he is flying home in a couple of days, he wants to see me, he is so sorry, he adores me, he wishes he could go back in time and regrets everything he said, they had all been selfish, we are family, and we should always stick by each other, through thick and thin. After his lengthy speech, I sigh loudly and embark on my own speech, insisting everything is okay, he is forgiven, everyone is, and this stress is normal given our abnormal circumstances, I cannot wait to see him, I adore him, too, and will pick him up from the airport, and the only way to proceed is by looking forward (the last part which is more directed to myself than to him or anyone).

MAMA'S HOUSE. Once I see the house, all my anger subsides. Yes, this may be denial. I do not care. I just want her to hold me. Oh no, Adam's car is here. I ask Alia if she mentioned to him that she was picking me up, and she says she has not spoken to Adam in a few days. "It must have been Mama," she says. "She was on the phone to him last night for the longest time," she adds. We walk toward the door. No need to ring the bell, it opens. Mom, Adam, and Alice are all here, hugging me, kissing my forehead. All of them have tears in their eyes. Crying must be contagious because I am crying again too and so is Alia. A houseboy peers from a living room and rushes toward me, shaking my hand, and starts crying, too.

We walk into the house. Mom leads me by the hand to the dining room. There is a breakfast feast laid out. Labneh and olives, zaatar bread, scrambled eggs, smoked salmon, fresh orange juice. I am not hungry. I had breakfast at the ward. But I do not want to break Mama's heart. I wish Baba were here. I cannot wait to see Yasser. I miss Layla. But I will focus now on this breakfast that Mom has prepared for me (or the feast that one of the chefs or both of the chefs have prepared for me).

Here we are, all together. The conversation ranges from "Here, have some orange juice" to "Pass the smoked salmon" to "There's a thunderstorm coming tonight, torrential rains." Adam is squeezing my hand. Electricity runs down my spine. How can I feel attracted to him when I am supposed to be upset at him for reporting me? How long has it been since we were last intimate? Best not to think about it right now. Is that avoiding my feelings?

After a full meal, we are sitting in the living room. Adam says he is running late for work and has to leave. He asks if I want to stay at Mama's or if I would like him to drop me home. I choose the latter. I am tired. I want to sleep under the covers of my bed. In my marital home. And when Adam comes home from work later, I want him to sleep beside me. I miss his touch. What is happening to me? I am supposed to be repelled by him for having me locked up.

Adam and I kiss everyone goodbye and walk to the car. He opens the passenger door for me. He is always respectful, yes, but he has never done this before. I know many women do not like these gestures because it makes them feel inferior or reminds them of the patriarchy, but I like it.

Adam starts the engine, turns it off, and starts bawling. His head is on the steering wheel.

"What's wrong?" He must feel guilty like Alia and Yasser.

"I'm so sorry, I can't do this right now. All I do is worry about you. I don't want to keep doing this to you, but I need time away. Maybe you can stay with your family for a while."

I cannot believe what he is saying. Here we go again. He seems to choose the most inopportune moments to tell me he is leaving.

And what is wrong with him? How can his temperament change so drastically from one moment to another? The chorus reminds me I am not one to judge. I am not judging. I just think he is unstable. Just like I am. Maybe he belongs in a psychiatric ward too. The chorus asks why I think so. For being a great pretender who cannot handle commitment, I respond. He came to my Mama's house, held my hand, hugged me, and acted as a dutiful husband—and now he is telling me he needs space? I cannot believe I was ready to be intimate with him again. Disgusting! Sickening!

"Why did you come to the house?" I ask picking at a stubborn cuticle.

"Your Mom and I spoke. She wanted to know why you haven't been in touch with me all this time. I don't know what to tell her."

"You don't know why? You had me admitted, Adam. I should be asking for time away, not you. You can't keep threatening to leave me. I am recovering now, slowly but surely, and I won't let you or anyone bring me down again. You're either in or out."

He explains why he had me admitted (as if the reason is not obvious to me, maybe I am giving him a hard time, it is not like he had any other option). He says he was worried. It was too much responsibility. What would he have done if I had killed myself? He does not mention whether he is in or out, and a paranoid thought surfaces in my mind: maybe he wanted to get rid of me and did not expect me to come out so soon, and now he cannot handle the fact that I am back.

"Does Mom know you want to leave me?"

"No, she doesn't. And I don't want to leave you. I just need time." Oh, what a coward he is! But maybe I am too much to handle. Maybe he is justified in wanting to be away from me. I can't even live with myself. I can't even handle myself. I want to run away from myself too. But I want to make him feel guilty. I want him to feel horrible for making me feel horrible about myself.

"You know what, Adam. Go to hell! I know this is too much for all of us to handle. But I'm tired of you making me feel like a burden. I'm so over our marriage dangling from a thread. Just take me home, I'll pack my things, and you can bring me back to Mama's when I'm done. I'm sure work can wait. And please divorce me right away." I know I could drive back to Mama's myself, but I am worried I may have a panic attack on the way back. I am glad Adam does not tell me he is running late again and cannot drop me.

I cannot believe what I just said. The D-word. Uh-oh.

"Dunya, you're overreacting. I don't want to divorce you. I just need time away."

I feel relieved he does not want to divorce me, or at least says he does not, but I am furious. And if he is going to threaten me with leaving, I will threaten him in return with divorce.

"Yeah, yeah, time. You said that already. Well, I'll give you all the time you need. You can have the rest of your life away from me. You can have forever. Is that enough time for you? I'm not going to sit here and let you mess with my heart. I don't want to walk on eggshells to keep you around. The last thing I want is a wishy-washy man. I'm not going to let my sanity depend on whether you want to stay with me or not. I have to take care of myself. Thank God I have my family now. And I have Layla, Alice, and Dr. Zahra. I don't need you or anyone else."

I ask him to start the car. I want to go home and get my things. We are driving home in silence. He is crying again. I want to hold him, but I hate him. He has no right to play with my feelings like this. Why is it so burdensome for him to support me? If he had publicly announced his atheism, I would have never threatened or even wanted to leave. If he had been imprisoned because of his announcement, I would have never threatened or even wanted to leave. If his family had abandoned him, I would have never threatened or even wanted to leave. If he had succumbed to one nervous breakdown after another, I would have never threatened or even wanted to leave. But he is not me. I am not him. And I guess he is not good at unconditional love. Not like I am.

HERE IS our house now. Adam runs out of the car and opens the car door for me. Does he think that by being gentlemanly he can absolve his guilt? I will not let him get away with this. I will show him. Adam tells me he will wait for me in the car while I pack. I cannot believe his nerve. Has he no feelings? He is staying in the car? He does not even have the decency to walk inside with me.

I walk toward the door and ring the bell. Jenny opens the door for me. I tell her to get me a suitcase and a pulley. She nods. Jenny brings the luggage to my room and tells me to lay my clothes and toiletries on my bed so she can pack them for me. I want to lie on the floor. I want Adam to curl up beside me and tell me he loves me and beg me to stay. I want him to come inside our room and just hold me. Oh, how I want him to hold me.

On the way back in the car, more silence. When we reach Mama's, Adam squeezes my hand, but I pull it away. What does he want from me? Why is he touching me? He says he will call me this evening. I tell him not to get in touch until he is ready to go to the divorce court.

"Divorce court? Have you lost your mind, Dunya? Please don't overreact. I don't want a divorce. Be reasonable."

I respond by getting out of the car, slamming the door, walking to the trunk of the car, and taking my luggage out. The gentleman does not even get out of his car to help me. I walk toward the door, dragging my luggage, and ring the bell. Alice comes out, tilts her head and raises her eyebrows. I cannot bear to look at her. She looks down at the suitcase and pulley and cranes her neck to look at Adam. I turn to look at him too. He has his head bent over the steering wheel. Alice sighs loudly. Sometimes there is no need for words. I hear Adam's car reversing out of the drive. I want him to stop. But he does not. I hear tires screeching. He is gone. My Adam. Gone.

I hear Mama say, "Who's there, Alice?" When she responds that it's me, Mom walks to the door.

She hugs me and asks me to tell her everything.

After explaining why Adam and I are not on good terms, Mom makes tea for us both and tells me that sometimes space is good. I tell her I want a divorce, and she says I am too angry to make any decisions now and that Adam is a good man.

"Don't let your anger at Adam dictate your life. Things will be resolved. A divorce is not the right solution at all. There's no rush to do anything. Stay here for now. Give Adam the space he needs. It's hard for men to express their emotions. He might be afraid to break down in front of you."

"He's my husband. I don't care if he breaks down. I've seen him cry. It doesn't make me see him as less of a man. Oh, I hate him, Mama. He keeps threatening to leave me. I'm tired."

"You know what Dunya? I regret every moment I spent away from you when I was upset. And in time, Adam will come to his senses and admit he made a big mistake too. Don't be like us, Dunya. Don't react like we do. We are all cowards. You're the one who is always here for everyone. You're just like your Baba, God bless his soul. You're the one who doesn't hurt people who hurt you. Let Adam see that. Don't hide your beautiful self from him because of dignity. That's never been your style, my love."

"I don't deserve this. I really—"

"Yes, I agree. You don't deserve this, but you can handle it. I know you can."

Somewhere inside me, the chorus, behaving in a nurturing way toward me, says, "See. That's all you needed. Your mom telling you she regrets abandoning you. Your mom telling you that you are always there for everyone. You are so beautiful Dunya."

Mom tells me she is going to take a shower. "See you in a bit, my love," she says, kissing my forehead. As she leaves, she adds that everything will be just fine, wait and see.

And I believe her. As I always have. But more than ever now. And I believe that nothing can cure a shattered heart like love. I do not need a diary, I do not need to vent, I do not need medication, I do not even need therapy. All I need is love. Okay, well maybe I need Dr. Zahra. Yes, Dr. Zahra *and* love.

ONLY FIVE hours ago, I submitted the article that I wrote in the psychiatric ward about mental health to a local newspaper. And I got a swift reply, saying they are afraid of backlash, and could I publish it under a pseudonym?

"Backlash?" I ask. "What's so controversial about the article?"

"Well," the editor responds, "the article isn't controversial. It's you, Dunya. It's your name. I don't think we can attach it to our newspaper."

"Ouch! That hurts," I want to respond. But the editor has already hung up on me.

I tried another newspaper, rejection. Another one, rejection. When I sent it to a newspaper abroad, they approved it within ten minutes. The article will appear online and in print in two days. Instead of rejoicing, I feel dismayed. When will my country have its faith in me restored? I promised not to write about apostasy and I will not. I learned my lesson although sometimes the chorus prods me to rebel. But how can I rebel? What is it that I want to write about? It is as though there is a topic lurking in my subconscious waiting for me to give it permission.

WHEN THE HABOOB SINGS

How can I give it permission if I do not know what it even is? *Come out*, I tell the article. *Come out so I can see you and decide for myself whether I will share you with the world.* Nothing appears. It will present itself when it is ready, the chorus states. For now, I am counting the hours and minutes left until I see Yasser. Three hours and thirty-three minutes.

WE ARE at the airport. I see Yasser. I run. I hug him. I hold him. I am afraid to let go. He twirls me around. We know we are making a scene, Yasser and I, but we do not care.

On our way out, a girl asks if she can take a selfie with me. I say yes. A crowd, of at least twenty people, surrounds me asking to take selfies with me. One of the men tells me he loves my work. A woman and what appears to be her daughter are hugging me. Alia and Yasser are smiling at me. As we walk toward the exit, they tease me all the way to the car: "Who's famous now? Huh?" Yasser asks, nudging me with his elbow. "You're a celebrity. Glad you have time for us," Alia says laughing.

When we reach the entrance to the airport, the driver comes running toward us and takes Yasser's luggage and walks ahead of us. My brother and I walk arm in arm all the way to the car. Yasser smells of Baba. I want to ask him if it is the same cologne, but I do not want to cry again. I am so tired of crying. I have become so sensitive. Just yesterday, I saw kittens in the house next door to Mama's and I bawled. This morning I cried during a commercial break. It was a commercial for an airline and a hostess was smiling at a passenger. Nothing worth crying about. Maybe something triggered inside of me. Who knows? Dr. Zahra tells me crying is cathartic, but it makes me more sad for some reason.

I kiss my brother's cheek. He has stubble. He tells me he had a beard, but he shaved it off a couple of days ago and it is growing back again.

We are on the way home. Alia is sitting in the passenger seat beside the driver, and Yasser and I are in the back, holding hands. He tells me about his boyfriend, Laith, and I see the driver look at him in the rear-view mirror. I nudge Yasser, and he says he does not care, Mom knows and that is all that matters to him. I find out his boyfriend is a local. I ask why his boyfriend lives in London, and he says he has a business there. But now, after falling in love with Yasser, Laith wants to move back here. He cannot wait for us to meet. I cannot either.

"Is he coming back soon?"

"Yeah, but first I'm going back in a couple of months. Then, I'll bring him back here so we can finally be together."

"Are you going to live with him here?" I ask.

"Yeah, but undercover. We're going to rent our own place."

"I thought they were cracking down on unmarried men renting bachelor pads."

"Well, it's not exactly like that." He looks outside the window. Alia turns around to look at me.

"Just tell her, Yasser," Alia says.

He looks at me. I look at both of them, waiting for someone to say something. I hate that they have become so close that they can keep secrets from me.

"What's up, Yasser?" I ask. His face is flushed.

"Well, I'm kind of getting married to Laith's sister, Fatma." He sighs.

"What? How? I don't get it. Why would you do that?"

"Look, it's an arrangement. Fatma never wants to get married. But she's getting a lot of pressure from her family. And she wants the freedom to go about as she pleases if you know what I mean."

"And what does Mom think? Does she know?" I have an obsession with Mom, I know.

"Yes, of course, she does. Mom was actually quite psyched when I told her," he says laughing. "You know how paranoid she gets about people gossiping. I'm sure most people in the family know I'm gay. But, nothing shuts people's mouths like conforming. I'll be one of them when I get married, so they won't care about my private life anymore. Mama can finally relax. And Laith and I can live together without anyone cracking down on us. And Fatma can break free. If that's not a win-win situation for everyone, I don't know what is."

I must look shocked because Yasser asks me why I am making a big deal about this.

"Oh, I'm not sweetheart. I'm so happy for you. I just don't know why you have to go through all this deceit to be with Laith. It's a bit extreme, no?"

"It's not deceit if all parties involved are aware. And I have friends who are in marriages of convenience and it works for them. The phrase arranged marriage is no longer what it used to mean."

Alia, Yasser, and I laugh.

"Well as long as you're happy, I'm overjoyed," I say to Yasser.

"Thank you," he says, squeezing my hand.

"Oh and congratulations. When's the engagement?" I ask, stifling a giggle. But Alia starts laughing and Yasser and I join in her laughter.

"When the time comes. No rush." He pinches my arm and leans over to kiss my cheek.

The driver brakes abruptly to avoid running over a man who crosses the street in front of us. The car swerves as the tires screech. Yasser puts his arm protectively across me.

"Go slowly, please," Yasser tells the driver.

"Yes, sir. Sorry, sir." The driver turns to face Yasser.

"Watch the road. Don't turn while you're driving. You're going to give me a heart attack," Yasser says. We all laugh including the driver, Abu. And then Yasser pats him on the shoulder. "I have missed you, Abu."

"Me too sir. Very much. Welcome home."

"Thanks."

At a traffic light stop, Yasser takes out a few notes from his pocket and places them in Abu's shirt pocket.

"Oh, sir. God bless you, sir. Thank you so much."

"So where is Fatma going to live?" I ask Yasser.

"With us. I'll look for a three-bedroom flat. One room for Laith and me. One for her."

"And the third?"

"For when guests come to stay. Or we might turn it into an office for Laith's business. We're not sure yet. We'll see how it goes."

"Do you smell something burning?" I ask Abu.

He begins to sniff. "No, madam."

Alia says it must be the smell of the tires from when the driver hit the brakes.

"Ah yes," I say. I see Abu nodding in the rearview mirror.

I ask Yasser what Laith's business entails.

"He owns a restaurant. It's called Lilacia. He's going to open a branch here. It's a fusion joint. It's a bit Italian, a bit French, a bit Spanish, a bit Greek. I guess you could call it a European bistro. You can check it out online. He has a website. The restaurant's a big hit. It's in Chelsea."

He sounds so proud. And seems so in love. I think of Adam. I wish Adam spoke of me in that way. I wish he had Yasser's look of love on his face when he addressed me.

"How did you meet?" I prod.

"We met at Alia's friend's dinner party in London. Oh, remember that night, Alia? You said the whole room could feel our connection. It was potent, right?" He leans over and rubs Alia's shoulder blade.

"Yeah, it was more than palpable," Alia says laughing.

It hurts me and strikes me as a bit callous that Yasser and Alia were falling in love and going on with their lives, distancing themselves from me while my life was falling apart. I will discuss this feeling of neglect with Dr. Zahra in our next session. I do not want it to contribute to another breakdown later.

WE ARE all together at Mama's house. Dad's ghost is here with us as we eat dinner. Dad is happy that we are all united and he is telling me to let go of the guilt I am feeling. Dad is assuring me he is in a better place. The chorus comes forth and is in a foul mood: "You're the reason your Baba is gone. Don't ever forget that. No matter what amends you make with your Mom and your siblings, you have to remember you're the reason your Baba is gone."

I start crying. Yasser and Alia exchange worried glances, and Mama gets up from her chair and walks toward me, stroking my hair. She asks me over and over again what is wrong. Alia says it is good for me to let things out. I tell Alia between sobs that I am anguished because I miss Dad, and I am upset that she and Yasser were having so much fun in London while I was in prison. Alia drags her chair close to mine and squeezes my hand and starts crying.

I am proud of myself for expressing how I feel. I am sure Dr. Zahra would be proud of me, too. But I feel guilty too. Why do I have to hurt people who hurt me? First Adam, now Alia and Yasser. I even hurt Mama by cutting my wrist right after seeing her. Mom is wrong when she said it is not my style to hurt people back. I hurt all of them.

Yasser is facing me. I look at him. He is mouthing *I love you* to me. I smile at him and wipe away my tears. I tell them I want to go to sleep, and Mama says that is a good idea. She calls Alice and they walk me to my bedroom. I go to the bathroom, lock the door, and wash my face, but I do not feel like brushing my teeth. I can hear someone knocking on the door.

"Are you alright, ma'am?" Alice asks.

"Yes, Alice."

I overhear Mom telling Alice to check if the door is unlocked. The knob turns. *Oh no, it's locked*, I hear Mom mumble. Does she think the door is made of steel and I cannot hear her? There is more knocking at the door.

I unlock the door. I walk out of the bathroom. My mom sighs in relief and hugs me. Alice brings me a pair of pajamas. I ask them to turn around while I undress and put on the comfortable tartan top and bottom I brought from the home I share with Adam, the home from which I have been banished. I sit on the edge of the bed. Mama walks toward me and tucks me inside the bedcovers. I will always be a child to her, and that is fine with me. Mama is stroking my hair.

I know that Mama and I will never break ties again, but one day I will have to face losing her, and I promise myself now, I vow to myself, that I will never allow myself to break down again or grieve for her the way I did for Baba.

Mom turns off the main light and keeps the bathroom light on. Alice says goodnight and they leave the room.

OH, I do not want Mama to die. How can I promise myself I will not grieve? How do I know how I will cope? The chorus tells me to stop thinking about death and coping. I turn on the bedside lamp, open my laptop. I have more emails. I cannot check them now. I go on Twitter. Again, there are too many tags to pay attention to right now. This is who I am. I am a writer, a famous one, and people from all over the world anticipate or dread my words.

Wait what is this? What is coming forth? Yes, here it is. Here is the article that has been lingering in the shadows of my subconscious. Here it is, finally, presenting itself to me. "Freedom of worship, Dunya," it commands. "That's your next article."

But I cannot write about such a thing. I will get into trouble again.

The chorus sings: But it's not related to apostasy.

Isn't it?

No, it isn't. Not exactly, that is.

Oh but it is! It surely is!

And without even thinking, the words begin to flow. I type faster than my thoughts. I ask why we think it is okay as human beings to tell each other what to believe in, and I ask why we do not have temples of worship other than mosques and churches in my country. Many religious people would argue that polytheistic religions should not be permitted in a country that adheres to monotheism, I write, but if that is the argument here, why are there no synagogues if even the Koran acknowledges Jews as People of the Book? And maybe our country should be secular, I write, so that we can see temples and ashrams and various sacred houses in our country, regardless of whether followers of a given religion believe in one God or many. Many of our neighboring Muslim countries permit temples. Are they more tolerant than we are? Why? I write and write and write some more. I write about giving expatriates the right to worship the way they give us the right to worship in their lands. When I am done, I move sentences around, check the grammar and punctuation one last time, and I remember my mother. With the apostasy article, she had wished I had run the article by her first. I will show it to her in the morning before submitting it. This is a vow I make to myself.

Everything is fine, I tell myself. I have my family. I have my writing. The chorus tries to remind me that I do not have Adam, but I am too excited by the article to care.

IT HAS been less than twenty-four hours since the article about freedom of worship has been published, and I have received countless emails. I read some of them with Mama. She is appalled by some of the angry comments. I tell her I am used to them. I am so glad this time I showed her the article beforehand and she approved it. In fact, she said it was beautiful, that my sentiments were beautiful, and that my heart is beautiful. Mom asks to see my website, but I tell her it crashed earlier today. And my computer is taking ages to load.

Mom leaves the room. I restart my computer. Oh, good, it is working now. There are more emails. I cannot keep up. It seems there are more haters than supporters this time.

Someone writes that I have an agenda to corrupt people. No. I have no agenda, I am not promoting anything, I am just asking for respect of others. According to most of the emails, my defense of atheists and polytheists is upsetting. One man says that it is one thing to defend apostates and infidels, but it is utter blasphemy to defend atheists. Apart from the scathing comments, I get the usual death threats as well. I read on. One man tells me I am a Zionist agent—yes, we love that accusation in this part of the world, anything that goes against the grain is called Zionism. Here is an email berating me, saying I am a product of everything that is wrong in the world today—yes, me, yours truly, it is all my fault the world is in a state of chaos. Oh, and in one email, someone points out a typographical error (a comma where a period should have been) in my article and asks me how a renowned Western paper could not have picked that up and maybe I should give up writing if I cannot even type a sentence properly. He adds that he will take a picture of my typographical error and post it to Instagram and expose me. To expose me? Is he for real? But real or not, this one strikes a nerve. He has hit at my writing. I check his email profile. No name, no photo—of course, just another troll hiding behind a screen. I want to tell him we are human beings, and no matter how much we edit or proofread material, typos slip through. I want to remind him that some of the most famous, bestselling books in the world have errors in them. But some people are just plain critical. I mean, do not get me wrong. I notice grammatical errors, punctuations slips, and spelling mistakes too. And if the author knows me personally, and asks me to look out for errors, I will inform him or her about them. Otherwise, I read on and enjoy the book. And if I do not know the writer, I do not bother getting in touch. I care too much about the message, what is being written in the article or the book. But some judgmental people lose the plot (sometimes literally) and scour for typographical errors out of contempt.

And who mentions a typo in an online review forum or on social media? That is sabotage. Why would anyone do that? Mistakes slip by even the most hawkish eyes. And typos can easily be fixed these days, but if an old review mentions a typo, a reader may think it is still there although it has already been corrected. Writers appreciate being told privately about their typos so they can fix them. Even Stephen King asks readers to report errors and typos found in his novels via a contact form on his website. And that is Stephen King! Yes, Stephen King himself, a prolific author who works with the best editors and proofreaders in the publishing industry.

I read some emails of support. One lady calls me a hero. A man says I have expressed his thoughts exactly. Most call me brave. You are brave, Dunya. That was brave. Bravo! Well done, you brave soul, you. The worst part about being famous is not being able to respond to all the emails. Even if I wanted to, I would not have the time. And I am tagged so much on social media, I cannot leave comments or thank my supporters.

Should I check whether the guy has posted the typo on social media? No. I should not. Why should I give him that satisfaction? But the real reason I do not want to check is I do not want to cringe in case he has mentioned it publicly. It is just an out of place comma, I know, but still...

I close my laptop. Enough hate for one day.

MISHAL THE lawyer, aka Skinny, calls to tell me there were people at the courthouse earlier in the day trying to file lawsuits against me. He says the judge shooed them all away. And in secret, the judge told Mishal the reason he got rid of them was that he was worried they would endanger my life and he wants to protect me.

"You're a lucky lady, Dunya," Mishal says. "Someone up in heaven is watching over you."

I start crying. Mishal asks if I am okay. I assure him that I am more than okay and that it is good to know there are people like the judge in power in this country. First, our ruler freed me from jail, and now a judge is protecting my life. If we had more compassionate people like them in power, our country could evolve, transform. Sadly, there are a lot of haters out to get me though. But no matter how hard I try, I cannot hate the haters. Nobody could ever hate me the way I have hated myself in moments of despair. Nobody has been meaner to me than the dictator in my head. And so by condemning haters, I am condemning myself. Still, I wish they would disappear, along with the hater in my head. I wish they would vanish into thin air. Poof! Goodbye haters.

I tell Mishal about the death threats.

"Dunya, send me their email addresses. That's sufficient evidence to indict them. We can track them down even if they have fake accounts. We have experts who can do that. In the meantime, before we find out who they are, my office will reply to each of them and send them a warning and ask them to appear in court."

I tell him to forget about it. "No, we cannot discard these death threats. We must take each one of them seriously. I can have them summoned to court or face consequences. We must take legal action against them or they won't stop."

"Thank you, Mishal, I appreciate it, but it's not important. I'm not frightened one bit. I used to be, but I have gotten used to them now. They're just trying to intimidate me."

"There are dangerous people out there. One of them could be out to get you."

"I think they're bluffing."

"Well, at least consider it," he says.

"I will," I lie, having already made up my mind.

"And, Dunya," he adds, "I know you haven't broken the law since you haven't mentioned apostasy, but this new article of yours is provocative. It's as though you are using any loophole to defy our society. Can you stay away from religion?"

"Yes," I say. And I will. I have already written the articles I wanted to, expressing more than I ever dreamed I could express in my country, my beloved country with its delicate minds and sensitive souls. And I will keep my promise to Mishal.

THERE IS an email from Adam. Oh. There are butterflies in my stomach but amazingly no tears.

> To: Dunya Khair
> From: Adam A.
> Subject: I miss you
>
> Dear D,
>
> It has been a while since we were last in touch. It's strange that I have to send you an email, but you're ignoring all my phone calls and messages. I didn't want it to get to the point where you're completely ignoring me. Oh God, I miss you so much. I keep wanting to come to your Mama's house, but I'm not sure how you would greet me. I know I asked for space so, in turn, I have to now respect your obvious need for space. I don't want to make a scene or anything like that. But I am dying to

see you. Anyway, please call me or at least respond to this email. I'm going crazy here without you.

I'm so sorry. I know I keep apologizing in my messages, but I owe you more than just one apology. I don't blame you if you have stopped trusting me. Sometimes I don't think things through. But I made a big mistake, and that takes a lot to admit, but I'm willing to beg to get you back.

I'm a miserable wreck. I have been since the first night we were apart. But, I was too ashamed to let you know, and one day passed and then another and another. And I lost count of the time we have spent apart, and here we are. I love you. I love you. I love you. I can keep on writing I love you all day and all through the night and it will never be enough.

What kind of a husband am I who runs away when the going gets tough? In a paradoxical way, it's a good thing I tried this, because I know I can never do this again. Ever. If you'll find it in your heart to forgive me, I'll come and pick you up right away and bring you back to our home where you belong.

I hope you have reconsidered getting a divorce from me. You know I never wanted that. I just wanted space. I hate that word now. Space? Was I out of my mind? Space from the most amazing woman ever? What an idiot I was. What an idiot!

I want to make you happy, and I can only do that by showing you how much I care. You were always a good wife. It was selfish of me not to be able to handle what happened. I should have been there holding you through your grief and pain.

Please answer this email. I beg you. Oh, by the way, I read both of your articles, the one about mental health and the one about respecting others' beliefs. Well done! I'm so proud of you. You are such a gifted writer.

So much love,
Adam

I TELL Mama about Adam's email. Of course, she tells me to work things out with him sooner rather than later, but I tell her I am not ready to see him or communicate with him. I like being in Mama's house. There is a part of me that wants Adam back, but I know it is not the right time. This separation has been good for me. I do not feel insecure in Mama's house. Adam made me feel unwanted, and now I feel liberated from him. Still, his email has made me restless. I call Layla and ask if she is free now. She says she will make herself free for me. She was supposed to go to her cousin's house but would much rather be with me. I tell her I will be at her place in an hour.

Alia drops me off because she is going to a supermarket next to Layla's house. She says she will pick me up in an hour.

At Layla's, we sit in the television room. Over a cup of jasmine green tea, I tell Layla about Adam's email. But she wants me to read it to her, word for word. I take my cell phone out of my purse and oblige. She asks me what I want to do. I tell her I will email him, but not just yet. When I am ready, I say. When I am ready.

To: Adam A.
From: Dunya Khair
Subject: I miss you too

Dear Adam,

I am sorry that it has taken me so long to respond. I just wanted to be in the right frame of mind, you know? Let me start out by saying thank you so much for your email. I read it over and over again. I know I will read it again after sending this. At first, to be brutally honest, I felt numb. I didn't feel like responding or even seeing you. But, somehow, a readiness to get in touch has been ignited.

I'm sorry that I keep ignoring your calls, but I am still upset at you, regardless of how much I love you. And though I don't want a divorce either (even though I said I did in a fit of rage), I am

WHEN THE HABOOB SINGS

not ready to come back to you. I don't know why, it's just something I have to trust. I've been quite impulsive, and my impulsiveness keeps driving me off the edge, so I think it's time to just sit with everything that's happened to me with you, Baba, my mom, Yasser, and Alia, and take things slowly.

I'm not saying this to punish you or to make you feel worse, but I think it was wise of you to suggest a separation. It came at the right time or was perhaps overdue. Sometimes things happen for the best, and God works in mysterious ways. It's no coincidence that you decided to leave me a couple of days before Yasser came back from London. I believe in divine timing, and this period is for my family and me. It was way too overwhelming having to juggle all my issues at once. I know that from experience now, and I cannot afford another breakdown, so I'm living from one moment to the next. To be honest, I could have worked things out with you before my family, but you kept shutting me out. You didn't even want to sleep in the same room with me for the longest time. And so I guess I'm meant to resolve things with Mom, Alia, and Yasser first.

I am seeing Dr. Zahra three times a week now. She wants to ensure that our separation and my moving back with my family will not affect me adversely. She also recommended a family therapist to resolve any underlying resentment and grief. My mom's not on board, but Yasser and Alia are, so we are starting soon. And she thinks you and I should see a marital therapist once a week if that resonates with you.

I can honestly say I am feeling better. Everything is being resolved. Our time will come, too, Adam. And I think therapy will help us both. I am finally beginning to see its positive effects on me. It's getting me to think differently. I am learning how to respond to situations rather than react. It's not easy, but I am committed to getting better.

I want to make sure that if and when another bout of depression hits, my main focus is making sure I don't harm myself. I am aware of how mentally unstable I was (and may still be, I'm not out of the woods yet) and how I put myself in dangerous situations when I couldn't cope. I'm still a risk to myself. I know that. And in order to avoid being sucked into a vortex again, I have to remain mindful and not overwhelm myself. Each decision I make now is weighed, however trivial. When it's time to eat, I ask myself if I am hungry or whether I am just eating because it's time to. Imagine that! If I practice with trivial things, decisions for weightier matters will come more easily.

It took me time to write this letter, because I wanted to make sure I was not answering you from an emotional or needy place, or out of a sense of obligation, but from a place that was ready to communicate.

Side-note: To be fair, I *am* feeling needy writing this to you, but I won't let my neediness make me impatient to return to you if that makes sense. I won't let my neediness usher me back to you until I am ready. Hey, maybe we can have coffee sometime soon?

Love,
D

HERE IS a response from Adam, a mere twenty minutes after I sent mine. This is the first time in the history of our relationship that we have emailed one another. How formal. I notice that, like me, he does not like replying to emails by hitting the reply button! We both prefer to compose an entirely new email. Is that weird or cute? Maybe he is just copying me. I do not know. But I am happy there is a new subject and he has not lazily hit a reply button. Am I obsessive-compulsive or what?

> To: Dunya Khair
> From: Adam A.
> Subject: Coffee! Yes!
>
> Dear D,
>
> That's a great idea. Coffee! Yes, for sure! Let me know when. I'm restless to see you, but I'll wait for a cue from you. I hope you believe me when I say I will never let you go again. Ever. God, I love you.

WHEN THE HABOOB SINGS

As for marital therapy, I think it's a great idea. Count me in! I'll do anything to fix things with you. Most couples want to go back to the way things were, but in our case, I want to go toward the way things *will* be. Things weren't good. I wasn't a good husband to you.

I'm not writing this letter to lure you back. I'm just telling you how much I want you back.

Every cell in my body is fighting for you, and there's not one thought in my brain that thinks I made the right decision in leaving you. Not one, D. I keep trying to rationalize or justify what I did, but I can't. And what does that tell you? Or what does that tell me? That I'm fully to blame.

I left when you needed me the most, and of that I'm guilty. And only I can rectify this. Only I can make sure this never happens again, baby. God, I love you.

Love,
Adam

I check the time. It has been forty minutes since Adam sent the email and five minutes since I have read it. Am I ready to respond? Or should I wait? I do not want to wait this time.

To: Adam A.
From: Dunya Khair
Subject: Thank you

Dear Adam,

I believe you when you say you won't ever leave again. And I know things will work out between us. We both want our marriage to work, and that's a recipe for success. I'm glad you agree to marital therapy. I think it would be best to see a therapist when I consider moving back, so I'll give you a heads up when the time comes. I'm starting family therapy in a couple of days, and I want to focus on that and my continued private sessions with Dr. Zahra for now.

Thank you for caring Adam. I don't mean that sarcastically in any way. I mean it as sincerely as possible. Truly. Thank you.

All my love,
D

WOW! JUST seven minutes later another response from Adam. Does he have nothing else to do but to check his email? I mean, I am flattered by his eagerness to respond but also irritated that he thinks he can speed up our reconciliation. Is that what he thinks he is doing? Or is that what I think he is doing? In any case, I admire his transparency.

> To: Dunya Khair
> From: Adam A.
> Subject: Coffee?
>
> Dearest Dunya,
>
> Yes, yes, of course I understand. There's no rush to see the marriage therapist. Also, I don't want to bother you, but you still haven't mentioned when we can meet for coffee. I'm impatient to hold your hand and kiss your forehead.
>
> All my love and more,
> Adam

I am not ready to tell him when we can have coffee. When will I be ready to have coffee? I know I am the one who suggested it. And I meant it when I wrote it, and I still want to see him, but I wrote *soon*, and he wants to know exactly when that will be. I will not let him pressure me. I will see him when I am ready. I close my computer. I do not feel like emailing him back now.

IN OUR session this morning, Dr. Zahra told me to consider speaking to Adam on the phone but only when I am ready. I like the way that she gently prods me to do things without pressuring me.

It has been three days since his email. He has tried to call and text me, but I have not answered him. I send a text to his phone asking if Tuesday is a good day (today's Sunday)—I am not ready to call him yet. He texts me back right away saying that Tuesday is more than good and asks what time.

How about 4:00 p.m.?
Brilliant. Where?
Zen Zone Café?
Done.
Okay, see you then.
Love you, D.
Love you too, Adam.

LAST NIGHT a violent haboob hit our country from the northest north to the southest south to the westest west to the eastest east. Not one part of the country was spared. It was surreal. Everything turned pitch black outside. We were all home except for Alice who was on her way back home from her day off and got caught in the middle of it. She called Mama from the taxi crying. Mom was emotional and passed the phone to me.

    I tried to calm Alice down, but she kept repeating *It's a sign. The end of the world is here.* Over and over again. Though she was being melodramatic, I must confess I had never witnessed a haboob that strong before. None of us had. The windows were rattling and black grains of sand were scattered all over the reception area of our house. The entrance hall and living rooms were enveloped in a surreal haze of dust. We had to put wet towels under the doors. According to the news, four people had died at sea. And there were twelve fatal car crashes and counting. The haboob left as abruptly as it appeared. And that was that.

I HAD a particularly enlightening session with Dr. Zahra two hours ago. We discussed my first family therapy session with Alia and Yasser. It was not tense at all for me, I told her, but awkward and traumatic for my brother and sister. Yasser cried, telling the therapist, Dr. Abdullah, that he cannot get over his guilt for abandoning me. And Alia could not look at me while apologizing, and when Dr. Abdullah asked her to look at me, she started bawling. He suggested that she write a letter to me or even write her feelings down in a journal. I remembered the diary I wrote in, or *to*, at the psychiatric retreat. I told Dr. Abdullah about it. He asked me if I was still writing in it and I said no. I used it in the ward as a form of therapy and said I had no idea where it was. He laughed. And Alia and Yasser laughed. And I laughed. When we came home, Alia said she would rather face me than write in a silly journal, and she looked right at me and said she was sorry. I was nervous and looked at the floor, but I felt happy. It was a strange sensation. All I could do was hug her. For the longest time.

IT IS a lovely evening for a walk. The sky is a canvas of pink and orange scattered with cottony cumulus clouds. I put on my ankle socks and trainers. I choose a salmon-colored T-shirt and gray sweatpants. My trainers are pastel yellow with white rubber soles. I look at myself in the mirror. I have gained weight at Mama's house, and I feel healthy. My face is glowing. Alia asked me a few days ago if I was wearing blush, and I said no. When I told Dr. Zahra that Alia thought I was wearing blush, she said it must be an inner glow radiating on the outside.

I walk toward the door. It is cooler than I thought it would be. I walk back inside, I remove my T-shirt and wear a thermal vest underneath and put on a caramel-colored hoodie. I go back outside. I feel a sudden pang in my chest. I miss Adam. It is not the time to cry right now. A walk will clear my head.

The breeze is picking up. I heard it might rain heavily tomorrow. Everything in our country comes to a standstill when it pours. Our highways get blocked, streets flood, sewage systems get clogged, electricity cuts off, and schools and offices close. It is not the amount of rainfall that brings the country to a standstill but our infrastructure. Our roads and cables are not well equipped to handle torrential rain. It has been an ongoing issue for years, and lately, the rain, along with the burden that comes along with it, has been getting heavier and heavier. But despite shuffling at the Ministry, resignations, forced retirements and pointed fingers, the whole cycle repeats itself when the next bout of heavy rainfall or a freak storm hits.

I keep walking. I check my wristband: four thousand steps since this morning. I will walk until I reach ten thousand steps. I hear footsteps behind me. I can feel someone close. I turn just as a man's shoulder brushes against mine. Now that is a bit too close for my liking. The man walks ahead of me. *Phew.* That was not pleasant at all. It is a suburban neighborhood, not an alley, and it is only 7:00 p.m., but one can never be too careful. I have heard murmurs of public sexual harassment in broad daylight, and though not commonplace in this country, or maybe underreported, the stories are enough to keep me on high alert. Sometimes it sucks to be a woman.

The man is a couple of steps ahead of me. He jogs farther ahead, stops, turns around, looks left and right and now straight at me. He is not going away, is he? He must be unstable or some kind of pervert. I have a sudden urge to call Adam. I take out my cell phone from the pocket of the hoodie and start to dial Adam's number, keeping my eyes on this stranger, who is taking something out of his pocket. And I see it, a shiny black object. It is facing me. I hear a loud sound. And another loud sound. One more time. *Pow! Pow!* This cannot be happening.

I feel a sharp pain in my chest. Oh, it is piercing and blood is gushing. My phone falls from my hand. I hear the screen crack. I fall to my knees. I want Adam, Mama, Baba, Yasser, Alia, Alice, Jenny, Layla, Dr. Zahra. I want Nurse Leah.

People come running toward me. Where were they before? One man, the hero of this scene, runs in the opposite direction after the man. They both disappear. Will he catch him in time? I hold the part of me that is hurting. It is sticky. I look down at it tenderly, maternally. When I look back up at the people around me who are trying to comfort me, I lose vision. I cannot see anything. I try to hold on, my eyes are open, but everything is black around me, although I can still hear sounds and voices. There are a lot of voices. Someone says: "Oh my God, it's Dunya Khair!" Another one says: "No, it isn't." I want to say, "Yes, it's me," but I cannot speak.

I hear sirens. There are hands on me and a burning sensation on my chest. Someone is tying something around me. I think it is a chest seal. I want to sleep, but he—or she?—wants me to say my name and is asking me where I live. They are trying to keep me awake. I know this tactic—I took a First Aid course once. It is dangerous for me to sleep now. But I want to go away from this planet. I am curious as to what is beyond this life. Is there something beyond? Am I about to find out?

Oh, my family will be heartbroken, but we all die. Death is a part of life. Adam will feel guilty for the rest of his life. I feel bad for him. I want him to hold me now. I want to tell him I have forgiven him and was ready to go back to him. I want to tell him he was the last person on my mind before... Before what? What happened? I cannot remember. I was walking. I remember that. What happened afterward? Stay awake, I hear a man say, and I want to tell him to hush, to be quiet, I am leaving and there is nothing they can do. I wish they could just respect my departure. Is that too much to ask? Am I going to make it? What if they save my life? Oh, perish the thought! Let me be! Let me be!

I AM here, not completely, but I am here. Am I not? Wait, where am I? I am moving, lying flat on my back. They are carrying me. I am on a stretcher. My eyesight is restored. I look around. Ah! I am in an ambulance. I close my eyes again. And open them. And close them. Now there are white lights, nurses in green, doctors in white lab coats. Why are there so many people around me? Where will I be when I close my eyes and reopen them? Will I reopen them again? The doctors are looking at me, I hear one shout: "Stat!" I want to tell them I am not afraid, I am ready to leave.

I am floating above the doctors and nurses. I look down at myself. Something hard is being pressed against my chest. I cannot feel it. I am near the ceiling now. But I can see my body jerk once, twice, three times.

I hear someone saying, "We're losing her." I say, "Look, I'm here." But nobody can hear me.

I read once that who we are at the time of our death is a defining moment. And here I am, a believer in God. An apostate, yes, but a believer. The chorus is singing, inviting me to sing along with it.

And we sing together: "La illaha illa Allah. There is no God but Allah."

EPILOGUE

From a personal blog
www.wonaibaranimodeerf.wordpress.com

It has been exactly one year since Dunya Khair's death. I have attended various vigils for her, a memorial service attended by thousands, and even a peaceful protest attended by media from all over the world. And, for the record, the majority of us present at the protest were locals and devout Muslims: Muslims who are tolerant of those who have different belief systems, Muslims who are perfectly okay with Dunya's apostasy and views, Muslims whose hearts break to see our faith hijacked by people who use it to justify their hatred and intolerance of others.

It is because of these people who have hijacked Islam that so many across the globe are afraid of us. It is because of these people that we, too, live in fear. It is because of these people who have attacked innocent souls in acts of cowardice and unfathomable violence that we are afraid to pray in mosques or wear attire that reflects our faith when we travel. It is because of these people that we are viewed as evil, even when we worship a Merciful and Compassionate God.

This morning, on the anniversary of Dunya's death, her killer was executed. Whatever our views are regarding capital punishment, any form of judicial retribution, whether by death or imprisonment, will never bring Dunya back to life. And our country is still in mourning. We came together as one in our country when Dunya died, liberals and conservatives. Even Members of Parliament who had fiercely opposed her mourned her death and released statements of condolences to her husband and family in local papers and on social media. That is the spirit of my country. Even when we disagree, we come together in tragedy.

His Excellency, the Amir, gave a speech about Dunya on television moments after the execution, saying she was a force for goodness and tolerance in our nation. And he ended his poignant and emotional speech by saying he will name the street on which she died after her. *Dunya Khair Street.*

I still cannot believe she is gone. May Allah have mercy on her soul.

ACKNOWLEDGMENTS

A shout-out to Sarah Spencer of Gatekeeper Press for all the brilliant work she has done on this book, from editing to arranging the book cover with the designer.

Here's to Hugh Barker, my first editor, for his unwavering faith in this book and his words of encouragement; to Brooks Becker, for polishing the novel with a magic wand. And to John Knight, a word wizard, for putting on eagle eye lenses. I curtsy to you all.

My gratitude extends to my flesh and blood and to all the souls who make my tail wag. How lucky am I to have built mansions in my heart for so many on this planet?

Finally, I would like to thank dust storms for reminding us that in one moment things can change.